T0065540

F**k God?

SPIRITUALLY TIRED, ABANDONED, DISCOURAGED, AND THE EFFORT DOESN'T SEEM WORTH IT?

Anthony Melvin

authorHOUSE®

AuthorHouse™
1663 Liberty Drive
Bloomington, IN 47403
www.authorhouse.com
Phone: 1 (800) 839-8640

Published by AuthorHouse 08/05/2016

ISBN: 978-1-5246-2342-5 (sc)
ISBN: 978-1-5246-2341-8 (e)

IT SEEMS LIKE YESTERDAY

For the first half of my life, I was a non-believer. Yes, I believed that God was real but that was about the extent of my belief system, "God was real." Instead of exercising a relationship with the actual living God and learning His Word, His ways, what He wants and expects of me, I was creating my own idea and image of how I wanted to see and view God. In my mind "God was this massive being who loved all of us and was everywhere, period!" Also, He was a personal genie who granted wishes and someone I didn't need to talk to but I could call on whenever I was in a crisis. Besides that, I never took my thoughts of God past that. Yes, there were plenty of times that I would question God because I wasn't seeing evidence of Him. I would later realize that it was not because I was not seeing evidence of Him, but that I wasn't seeing proof of Him that I wanted to see. Instead of me trying to come up to His way of thinking, I wanted to bring Him down to my way of thinking. I had no clue as to what speaking to God or God speaking to me really meant. But I will say that when God started speaking to me, it was like having a loud radio in my home, car, job and everywhere else I went, I just couldn't turn it off. I unplugged it, disconnected the wires, and smashed it with a hammer but that radio just kept blaring loudly!

I had no idea who Jesus really was. Because I was ignorant of the Bible and never exercised the Bible or the teachings of Jesus, I trivialized the Bible and God. "Jesus wasn't the son of God," I would say. "He was just a preacher who walked the streets claiming he was the son of God. Besides, we are all God's children, right?"

"I'm just as much a son of God as he is." I never understood when Christians would say things such as, "He died for our sins." Or the significance of the cross or what they meant when they said, "He rose in three days?" I would also ask, "If God really cares about us then why are there so many bad things happening in the world, and why do good people get killed every day?" I especially thought it was stupid that these Christian people would follow some TV preacher who claims that he 'speaks to God?' I would think, "You people are all idiots!"

Because I was ignorant of Biblical teachings, I did what I usually did during that era when I was ignorant of something or a subject; I talked, criticized and made a judgment about the Bible and Jesus based on what I thought I knew. This in retrospect was worth about fifty cents. But I never had a thought based on what I actually exercised or studied. Because I never applied the teachings of the Bible or Jesus' word, I didn't have a spiritual ground to stand on. So my ignorant, judgmental attitude about the Bible and Jesus continued. Also because of that mindset, I would minimize the Bible that was full of next level power down to a simple book that was nothing more than guidelines on how to live. "I don't need to read this book to know that I shall not steal, lie, be an adulterer, hate, and to love my neighbor. I don't need to read, study or exercise the Bible that was written by man anyway to know that. Sure, I'm not perfect, but I'm a nice, caring person who tries to help others when I can, and I give my spare change and my leftover food to homeless people when I come out of the store or restaurants. I'm a nice person who prays." I'll never forget what God said to me years later, "There are millions of people in the world who are nice, but who don't have a relationship with Me. There are millions of people in the world who pray to Me but don't have a relationship with Me." His words hit me like a ton of bricks. He was right. I prayed a lot, but I didn't have a relationship with Him. While living in Vegas, my neighbors were some of the nicest caring people that I ever met. They were always smiling, and the wife even collected clothes for the homeless shelters. I never heard them cuss nor have I heard them say anything that would be considered negative. However, they were Satanist who openly worshiped and prayed to Satan.

Since neither of us was exercising our relationship with God, what really separated them from me?

I CAN WORSHIP GOD
IN MY OWN WAY

I spent a lot of time talking about what was wrong with the churches in America and its members. When I would channel surf and come across a Christian program on TV, I would think that church people were weird and simple minded because they were waiting for a fake money hungry preacher to tell them what to do or how to think. "If they were really smart, had insight, and weren't so weak minded they wouldn't sit there like idiots letting someone else tell them who to be or how to think," was my way of thinking. "I don't need to go to a church, God is all around us, and I can worship Him in my own way. Plus, I got eyes, I can read the Bible myself if I wanted to; I don't need someone telling me what it means." What I didn't know at that time was these believers weren't sitting around waiting for some man to tell them who to be or how to think. They were actually there to be educated on the things of God. They were there to go to another level spiritually and more important, they were there to learn how to tap into the Christ power that envelops around them daily. At that time, I just didn't understand that. I didn't know what it meant to be under an anointed man of God. According to my self-righteous know it all attitude, if I wanted to learn how to fly a 747 jet, I didn't need to go to pilot school or be under a teacher with years of experience with knowledge and understanding about the ins and outs of that big flying machine. I'll just jump in the cockpit and fly it based on what I think I know about what it means to operate and handle a 747 jet. For you movie buffs, it's just like the world of Star Wars. Imagine someone who has no idea about how the force works, what makes it work or where its essence comes from. And instead of trying to learn and be under a spiritual Jedi master like Yoda, this individual decides in his own ego and arrogance that he understands more than he does. He doesn't need to be under an anointed teacher of the force. Because he trivializes what he doesn't understand and doesn't have the proper spiritual guidance to the power that he's trying to activate, it just won't work for him. He'll be trying to move objects with his mind without a source to draw from. That person was me; Full of arrogance.

SATAN WAS SPEAKING THROUGH ME

I was full of man-made wisdom, I studied different areas of psychology, Western philosophy, and parapsychology, so I believed that made me a student of real life and that I had a real open mind of the world. I never missed a chance to verbally try and put Christians, Catholics, Jehovah witnesses, church folks and other religious groups in their place or mock their way of thinking when the opportunity presented itself. I was trying to impress people who were spiritually endowed with man-made wisdom and believing that I was actually leaving an impression. When in reality and retrospect all I was doing was showing my ignorance.

Years ago on one of my jobs, I worked with a Christian woman. She was a humble woman and apparently strong in her faith. I waited for an opportunity to put her belief system down and to tell her what was wrong with her way of thinking, and one day the opportunity presented itself. When Jesus told Peter that, "Satan is speaking through you," in retrospect I knew that day Satan was speaking through me. I could feel myself being controlled and manipulated. I began to lay into her about her Christian faith and what I saw as obvious flaws and contradictions.

Then the most amazing thing happened, no matter what I was hitting her with she had a spiritual calmness and an insightful enlightened ready answer without effort. My verbal attacks to bring her down and to shake her foundation weren't working. I could feel the devil inside me becoming agitated so I came at her even harder; I was throwing man-made wisdom at her, attacking what I considered to be holes about her Bible, Jesus, and foolishness about her faith in general. She didn't even break a mental sweat. Without missing a beat, wisdom and power came out of her mouth, the

Holy Spirit was speaking through her as faith-filled words and biblical truth hit me like a baseball bat. When I realized that I had failed and was no match to challenge this woman of God, in the end, she had put the devil in his place and sent me away with my tail between my legs. All of the man-made wisdom I was full of was no match for the power of God that was working through her. At that time, I didn't look at that experience as a lesson or even try to absorb or consider what she had said. Instead, I took it as a challenge to be better and stronger for the next time I mocked and challenged a person of faith.

YOU'RE ALL HYPOCRITES! AND THAT MAKES ME BETTER THAN YOU!

Do you know one way to tell when a person doesn't have a personal relationship with God or even knows what they're talking about when they speak of the Bible or the things of God? When they continuously talk about what preachers, Christians, and believers are doing wrong and the hypocrisies in the church. That person was me. The main thing I targeted was the hypocrisy in the church, among Christians and other believers. I went out of my way to always point out the two-faced believers, liars, and self-righteous. This type of behavior and hypocrisy from them to me only validated my stance as to why their way of thinking and belief system didn't work. It would be years later that God would speak to me about this. He said, "Do you really think I care about your judgmental opinion about what some of My believers are doing wrong. Did I ever ask you your opinion about them or am I more concerned with you exercising and strengthening your relationship with Me?" He went on to say, "How is it, that by you worrying about them brings you closer to Me? How can My power even begin to work in your life when your focus is in the wrong place? You continuously put down others and point out their faults to mask your own insecurities and shortcomings. Your heart being in the wrong place only hurts you, not them."

MOMENT OF TRUTH

Because I was ignorant of the teachings of the Bible, I always assumed that God was really a stiff who only helped and worked through people who were righteous, holy, clean, calm, upstanding, and pompous if you will. At least that's what I saw on TV while growing up. It wouldn't be until years later while studying the Bible that I would learn the truth and that it was backward. God constantly helped and worked through people who were sinners, non-believers, people who were doubtful, people who mocked Him, or in some cases people who weren't spiritual at all. In other words, people like me.

One day, while I was challenging and criticizing people of faith in my own head, God caught me off guard with a question - a question that I had no immediate answer. He simply asked me, "Can you tell Me in your heart of hearts that you've actually exercised what My son has taught in the scriptures?" I stopped for a moment and thought about what He just asked. I was about to lie and say, "Yes I have," to save face, but I didn't. I mean you can't lie to God, right? Instead, I asked Him, "What do You mean exactly?" He said, "Have you ever studied what My son Jesus has taught and exercised it? Have you ever put yourself in a position to find out if My power is actually real?" At that moment, my only answer was, "No." That's when it hit me like a ton of bricks. I had spent so much time reporting negative things about something I didn't understand that I forgot to actually do one thing to back up my reports. I forgot to do investigative journalism. After all, that's what a good journalist does, right? They investigate the story before they just report it. They go out and try to find substance to back up what they're claiming is fact, good or bad, to validate what they're saying.

Well, it turned out that God wasn't gonna' wait any longer for me to come to Him to investigate whether I thought His power was real. Instead, He did what He does best to non-believers; He put me in a position to where I would have no choice but to cry out to Him. He put me in a position to where I would have to stretch my hand out to Him to stop the pain. And let me just say that reaching out to and getting closer to God through my suffering, and I stress the word suffering, wasn't an easy thing to do at all. God had put me in a place of mental, emotional and spiritual suffering where the only way out was through Him.

It was a place of darkness and hopelessness, my wilderness experience. It was so bad that I thought that dying would be a better alternative than going through what I was going through. And I have to say that I never want to go back to that place again. But how else was I gonna learn? How was God gonna show how much He loves me and wants to be the center of my life unless He could show me that He can rescue me and pull out of the deepest darkest pit. He had to let me fall into the darkness so He could show me His light. Moreover, when I came out, I was an entirely different person. The final report was that this Bible/God/Jesus believing and praying thing is real! It's not a fairytale, it's not make-believe. But the living God, His power, and the Holy Spirit are real and alive in all of us!

CONNECTING THE DOTS

What I had learned throughout that process of exercising the Bible, Jesus' words, learning from an anointed teacher and last but not least, God truly revealing Himself to me, was that the living God wasn't just some being that was up in the clouds or far away from me, He was right there next to me the whole time. Yes, I had many spiritual experiences while growing up and had seen a lot of things spiritually that would probably scare most people. But the difference was during those times I didn't understand how it related to God or how to connect it to God and His plan for my life. During those times, they were just random spiritual experiences to me that added up to nothing. But the more God revealed Himself to me I began to understand my past and present experiences and things about myself. When they said, "God is all around us" they weren't lying. He wasn't hiding anything from me, and He would answer any question I had. I learned that finding God and talking to God was the easiest thing in the world to do. I just had to do it.

I GOT THE POWER!

My whole world changed once I discovered that God and His power was real in my life. Not trying to be funny, but yes, I felt like Bruce Almighty. I GOT THE POWER! I had learned how to tap into the power, pray, talk to God and how to listen and receive. I had gone from a man who had criticized everything about the Christian lifestyle to becoming a man that everything I touched turned into gold through God.

I could lay hands on people and heal through the power. I could pray for other people, and they would get instant results. I could ask and pray on my behalf and get a supernatural breakthrough in a blink of an eye. All I had to do was ask a question and wisdom and knowledge would come to me through impression. Sometimes before I would even finish asking the question the answer was given to me. God began talking to me so much and filling me with so much spiritual wisdom that sometimes I would have to pull the car over or while walking, go sit down and say to God, "Enough! It's too much. My mind is overloading." The bottom line is, when it came to God working His power in my life, my cup wasn't just overflowing, I couldn't even turn the faucet off.

But everything comes at a price. There was no denying it; everything I had heard about "God's power" working in our lives was real because He was working through mine and then some. But God had also shown me that soon it was all going to stop, at least temporarily. Because now that I had gotten a small taste of whom He was and what He was capable of doing in my life, like a credit card company, He was sending me a bill. When I got that bill, in my young mind at that time, I didn't know how I was going to pay it? The bill was huge. It was everything that God expected of me as a person, His son, a Christian, a man of God, a follower and a believer. All I could do was stare at it, not truly knowing if I was capable of actually paying it off. God even offered to allow me to start by paying it off in small payments - a little at a time. But it still seemed like a lot to pay off, even in small payments. In short, God was asking me to give myself and my life to Him. At that time, it seemed like a lot of Him to ask of me. I didn't know how to respond or if I wanted to respond at all. It was like driving a brand new sports car. I loved the idea and the luxury of driving it, looking cool in it, feeling the wind in my hair with the top down and impressing the girls as I drove by with the music blasting. But in the end, I didn't want the responsibility that came with owning the sports car, the monthly payments, the insurance, the maintenance fees and the tune-ups. I was at a serious crossroads in my life. I had a big decision to make. And that decision was God's way - or my way. I chose the minor. Though I was shown and exposed to so much next level spirituality, I felt I just wasn't ready for that type of spiritual responsibility at that young age. The responsibility scared me.

I BECAME A PART TIME CHRISTIAN

I had it all. The power was alive in me and so was His favor. But when I ran from my responsibilities, things began going downhill for me. No, my life wasn't turned completely upside down, and God didn't entirely forsake me. But it wasn't the same as it was when I was overwhelmed with power and favor. And I was suffering the consequences of living the life of a part-time Christian. It showed in my conversations. I would complain and say things like, "If I am so favored and loved by my Father in heaven then why have I had more unanswered prayers and have felt so forsaken more times by Him than I can think of?" And, "Why does it feel like my Father in heaven hasn't been there for me when it really counted?" But the truth is, He was, and I was just too blind to see it. He was showing me a lot of signs and evidence of His work and help in my life; it just wasn't the evidence that I wanted to see. I guess I know that if any of us want to see God's real power working in our lives, we have to exercise what Jesus and the Bible teach us and truly give all of our life to Him. Can I honestly say that I've not just read but continuously exercised the scriptures and the word of God in the Bible in my life? No, I can't. After all, I know what's relevant to me might not be relevant to Him. His ways aren't our ways and what man holds in high regard God usually detests. Or maybe because I believed that I was a caring, giving, good hearted person and because of that good things should've been happening for me and around my life. That seems fair right? But deep down I knew I still wasn't doing what I was supposed to be doing or lining up with His plan or His will in my life. I was trying to find a loophole. I was trying to figure out a way to get the blessings, favor, and power in my life while at the same time not being fully committed.

My friend Dawn once asked me, "Anthony, have you ever stopped and just asked God what He wants out of your life and you? Have you ever once said God take full control of my life and guide me into the direction You want me to go in?" Again, the answer was no. I guess I always felt His plans for my life might interfere with my plans for my life. "Am I wrong to feel that way?" I thought to myself, "He created me, right? He's the one who put all of my parts together and wired me this way, right? He knows He endowed me with initiative, goals, ambition and the drive to keep pushing forward. He knows He wired me to be creative and have constant ideas running through my mind. He knows the passion that I have. So am I wrong when I try to take the gifts He's given me to make something out of myself and my life?" I suppose the obvious answer was yes, yes when you don't exercise your relationship with Him or give God His due throughout the process. When you don't share with Him daily what you're doing or going through, good and bad or even pray or ask Him how He feels about what you're involved in. Whether it be finding a new church home, choice of job, finding a mate, choice of diet, entertainment, or just flat out having conversations with Him throughout the day.

So many times I have said to God, "God, I've made the sacrifices, paid my dues and did my part, how come You're not doing Your part? Why can You help me in this area in my life but not in this other area where I feel I really need Your assistance? Why do You choose to visibly intervene in some parts of my life instead of others? How come You choose to bluntly be in my face when I didn't ask You, but sometimes You seem slow to respond when I cry out to You? Why does it seem like I see more evidence of the devil than I see of You? I'm a good person, I don't deserve this!" One day He answered those questions and said, "Maybe I want more from you than just being a good person. I want you!" It's not always easy to hear the truth, because the truth hurts, especially when it doesn't fit your plan.

I began to wonder what He would do if I continued to sin and not listen to Him - If I continued to put Him on the back burner. How many times could I take Him for granted until He completely ties His hands with me and says, "No more, you've had plenty of chances to get right and build a relationship with Me. Your consequence has come." Even the Bible teaches that there will come a time where Jesus will close the door and say to the people reaching out to Him, "I don't even know you." Honestly, that scares me very much. Can you imagine experiencing the worst fear and torment you've ever experienced, and while going through it, Jesus Himself rejecting and not helping you because of all your years of rejecting Him? I actually visualize trying to climb out of a hot pit and reaching my hand out to Jesus and Him turning away and closing the door - completely forsaken by Him. To me, that is the scariest feeling in the world.

WHY ME?

I cannot count how many times I've cussed God out and said horrible nasty things against Him and Jesus. I'm talking about throwing full F-bombs at Him. I've spent a lot of years being angry at God and to put it lightly, "cursing His name" for what I call being an absent God.

Depending on the day you caught me, I can be the most spiritually enlightened person being overwhelmed with God's wisdom and knowledge you'd ever met. Or I can be an immature whining brat who's always asking, "Why is this happening to me?"

I can admit there were plenty of times where I felt like I was doing God a favor by attending church and praying to Him. I treated church like it was a time clock and by me punching in and out and making an appearance, I thought God should just be content and happy with my attendance. And even though I wasn't giving Him my best, I would bitch and complain when He wasn't giving me His best. On Sunday morning, I would be at church looking at my Bible and full of the Holy Spirit, but by Sunday evening, I would be out acting a fool.

Once I asked my Christian friend, "How come God has shown us strong evidence of His power, mercy and love in our lives, but we as Christians continue to openly sin, disregard, and take Him for granted?" Her response was, "That's the million dollar question, and when you figure it out you let me know." Of course, I know what the Bible says about sin, how we all for short, how Satan continuously whispers in our ear and how we must overcome the flesh daily. Still, I wondered in my own life how God can reveal Himself to me in HD, and I can still turn the channel on Him to see what else is on?

UNTIL THEN

While talking on the phone with my friend Dawn one afternoon, she asked me "Anthony, do you know how many Godly spiritual people will live their whole lives and never have the spiritual experiences or see the things that you have?" I paused for a moment, and then responded "No?" I suppose I never gave it that much thought.

As a Christian woman, my friend Dawn radiates favor and is blessed by God. When she speaks, I listen, and I'm always reflecting on spiritual conversations we've had, even if they were conversations we had years ago I still reflect on her words. She makes me think. She's giving, very caring and can educate about the things of God without being judgmental. Sometimes I think she doesn't even know how powerful or how gifted she really is when it comes to the things of God. Moreover, of course, when I say powerful/gifted I mean how God works through her. I'm sure most of us know of or have a Dawn in our lives who we count on for spiritual support and knowledge/guidance when we get a little bit off track which for me was all the time. As a friend, she really is something else. She has been my unpaid spiritual therapist for years, and I'm grateful that God has brought her friendship into my life. But on this day she asked me a question that not only seriously got my attention but had me staring at the ceiling at night for months, "Anthony, do you know how many Godly spiritual people will live their whole lives and never have the spiritual experiences or see the things that you have?" I didn't know how to answer.

"What does it all mean?" I asked myself. "Why do I continuously have these experiences of being protected, watched over and favor from God if you want to call it that?" Sometimes I don't know if I should feel blessed or confused. Either way her question stumped me.

Because of my spiritual experiences and insight does that mean that there's more expected of me? Does God have a real purpose for me being this way or are my experiences just a fluke?

I've had a lot of spiritual experiences, good and bad. But personally, I don't really believe that my experiences are that unique at all. I believe we're all surrounded by angels, spirits, and above all God's love and mercy. Maybe the difference is in my case as many other spiritually sensitive people are that I've just had the benefit to witness them. And whether it was selfishness or just plain ignorance on my part so many times in the past I would tell God, "You've got the wrong guy!" I know it seems silly to say that when He's the one who created me and knows the number of hairs on my head. But sometimes I would feel as if He's made a terrible mistake. There's an old saying, "My blessing is my curse," and sometimes that's how I would feel.

All I can say now is I'm thankful that He gives us the grace and time to grow and evolve spiritually; which is what I have done. Moreover, I'm happy to share my experiences with you.

I always knew that someday I would die; I just never
thought that it would be in my lifetime...

1

EVEN ANGELS CAN HOLD THEIR BREATH UNDER WATER

On a beautiful sunny afternoon in the summer of '79, in the city of Anchorage, the family was enjoying spending time together at Goose Lake. My mom had laid out a beautiful blanket and picnic for the kids. We ran around in the sand, played fun games like tag and had the time of our lives splashing each other in the water. It was a perfect day to be a kid.

I remember being jealous watching the older kids being able to do things in the water that I couldn't. They could hold their breath under water longer. They could do hand stands. They could also swim without splashing water everywhere. They were going into deeper water. I was doing pretty well to keep up with them the best I could, but I could feel my heart beating faster from fear. Still, I had to get to where the fun was at. The water was rising up on me and getting closer and closer to my chin. I would even have to swallow a little bit, but I was getting closer. None of the older kids were even paying attention to me as they went on with their activities. I figured when I got close without drowning myself, I could call out to them to grab me, which is what I did but they left me behind.

As my older brothers, sisters and cousins swam away from me, I began to feel abandoned and sad. They were going further out to have more fun and because I was small and only five years old I couldn't go where they were going. I started to cry. I made my way back to the sand. I sat on the edge of the water watching the older kids in the distance having their fun without me. "How could they leave me behind all by myself? Do they not see that I'm crying and hurting because I have no one to play with?"

I decided to do something about it. I was going to get back in the water and go out to where the older kids were. Slowly walking back in the water, I didn't know if I could make it to where they were or not. I didn't know how to swim or even doggy paddle. I turned around and looked at the surface one last time and then went for it; I was going to go in the deeper water.

Then something horrible began to happen. I could feel my feet losing ground. There was no warning; the ground just dropped off. I tried my best to hop up and down and each time my head went above water I yelled out to the older kids who couldn't even hear my screams of terror. I was in a horrible panic. I managed to turn around to see land, and that's when I saw something so amazing; long white legs running towards me and fast on top of the water. It was my mother. However, I was so tired and had used up all of my strength and energy. Finally, I just let go and submitted to the deep water and went under.

I was under water and my eyes were wide open. Odd, my vision wasn't blurred or obscured at all and I could see everything clearly and perfectly. It was like looking through glass. Also, my mouth was open, but I wasn't swallowing or drowning from the water. I saw a man underneath the water with me. What I remembered about him was he glowed and had a radiant smile on his face. He didn't speak, but through his smile, he was telling me that everything would be alright as he held onto my waist firmly. I wasn't surprised at all to see him; I was just happy that someone was there with me while I was going through this ordeal.

The man in the water continued to just smile at me. It was like his eyes were saying, "I love you and will always protect you." Then he looked up at the water's surface, and it became dark from whatever was above us. Still holding onto my waist, he hoisted me upwards; that's when I felt a hand grab my afro and pulled me up. When I surfaced from the water, I saw sunlight again and my mom's scared face. She hugged me until I couldn't breathe.

Even today, I still remember that man's smile from under the water.

Best friends for a season or best friends for life. Either way, I'll never forget you.

2

I MISS YOU TOO

Later, that summer of '79, I was outside learning how to ride my bike. I looked so cool riding down the sidewalk really fast with the wind whipping through my hair and breaking sound barriers. I was jumping over cars and doing cool wheelies. I was the envy of all the other kids in the neighborhood; at least in my own head. The reality was, even with the training wheels that were on my bike I was still struggling to keep my balance. Also, I was a nervous wreck.

After awhile, I had gotten a little bolder and decided that it was ok for me to stray away from my apartment building and began riding around the block. I was a little scared to stray away without anybody around to watch in case something bad happened to me. However, at the same time, I wanted to impress the people on the next block with my cool new wheels.

As I continued to ride down the sidewalk, I noticed a big mean looking dog heading in my direction. I didn't know if this dog wanted to eat me or just play, but I wasn't trying to find out what its intentions were. I began to peddle faster, and the faster I went, the faster the dog came towards me. I rounded the corner but didn't have enough time to slow down so losing my balance on the curb I fell over and hit the ground, hard. Like a criminal trying to leave the scene of the crime, the big dog took off when I started screaming and crying in pain.

I sat on the sidewalk crying with the bike over my leg. My leg and arm were cut. I also realized that I wasn't within screaming distance from my home. So, nobody there was coming to rescue me. When I began to realize that nobody was coming to help me, I pulled the bike off my leg. When I tried to get up it hurt too much to walk so I sat back down on the sidewalk and cried some more.

A woman approached me. She looked about mid-twenties. She was a brunette and had the most beautiful smile I had ever seen. She knelt down and touched my arm and said, "Don't cry. It'll be alright - let me help you." She picked me up and carried me into one of the single floor apartments nearby. We entered through the patio door. At that point in my life, I didn't know much about not talking to strangers or going into their homes. I was just happy that someone was paying attention to me and helping me with the pain I was going through.

She sat me on the kitchen counter, that's when I saw another woman who was blonde enter the apartment. She had brought my bike over from the sidewalk. She too had a beautiful smile. "You're so handsome," the blonde said to me as she approached me. "Are you hungry, would you like some cookies?" she asked. Of course, I was never one to turn down cookies. As she reached into the cabinets to grab the package of Fig Newtons, I noticed something very odd about the blonde woman; her physical presence began to fade in and out. First, I could see all of her and then maybe just a little bit of her. At that moment, I just let it go. She handed me the cookies, and that would begin my love for Fig Newtons, even to this very day. Both women were really pleasant to me.

The brunette haired woman continued to work on cleaning my leg. She kept looking me in the eye instead of my injury as if she already knew what she was doing. She also smiled at me the whole time. It was nice to get so much attention and be nurtured, even if they were strangers.

She put a bandage on my leg and lifted me off the counter to the floor. "It will heal," she said to me with her pleasant voice. Both women walked me to the patio door. They both hugged me, and this time, as I was saying goodbye, I noticed that both women's physical appearances were fading in and out.

Then the brunette haired woman knelt down in front of me and said, "Anthony, tell your mom that I miss her too." I turned away and walked my bike home.

At that time, I had no idea of what she meant by saying, "Tell your mom I miss her too." I guess I really didn't care or didn't know any better.

I went home to show my mom the scars. I told her about the nice ladies who helped me and bandaged me up. She was happy that someone was there to help me in my time of need. Then, I told her what the dark haired lady said, "Mom, she said that she misses you too." My mother stopped what she was doing, paused for a moment, turned around and looked at me. In her concerned voice, she said "What?" I repeated myself, "She told me she misses you too." I could still hear the woman's voice in my head saying those words to me. "What did she look like?" she asked. "Like you," was my answer about all women who had dark hair like my mom. "Anthony, are you sure that's what she said?" I nodded yes.

My mom wanted to know what the hell was going on, so she had me take her back to the apartment where the mystery ladies had helped me. When we arrived, we could hear a lot of activity and loud talking inside the apartment. My mom knocked on the door and a man with the biggest afro I had ever seen answered the door. Instantly we saw a bunch of guys in the living room watching a basketball game and drinking beer. The host was smiling when he saw a beautiful young woman at his door. "Hey, what's goin' on," he said. My mom asked him if there were two women living there because they helped her son earlier and she just wanted to thank them. "My wife is here," he said. He asked his wife if she had helped me earlier today but she replied no. My mom looked down at me and asked if I was sure this was the right apartment, I told her yes it was. I even saw the package of Fig Newtons still sitting on the kitchen counter. I remember wanting more. In a last ditch effort, my mom said, "My son says they were two white women," but the man was still clueless about the situation. She thanked the man and left.

A couple of nights had gone by; my mom hadn't let the situation go and was still not convinced that we had gone to the right apartment. I was taking a bath and when I got out of the tub and put my clothes on I heard her voice calling me from her bedroom. When I arrived, I saw that she had the photo albums out on the bed. She showed me three pictures. The first picture was of five women with their arms around each other in an obvious drunken state. My mom said to me, "That woman with the dark hair who helped you a few days ago, do you see her in this picture?" Without hesitation, I pointed to the woman who I knew to be her. She showed me another picture with multiple women in them and again I pointed to the woman in the picture I believed to be her and same with the third picture. I chose the same woman in each picture and recognized her as if she were still in front of me.

My mom sat back for a moment. Her eyes began to tear up. I still didn't know what this was all about. She leaned forward and grabbed her little magic box from the side of the bed and began rolling a joint (next to her children pot was her first love.) She said to me, "The woman you saw in the pictures was my friend, Janice. She was like a sister to me. She died in a car accident four years ago. You were only a year old when it happened. A week ago I visited her grave and put a card on her tombstone. Inside the card I wrote in big words, 'I miss you, Janice.'"

3

OUR GRANDPARENTS ARE ALWAYS WATCHING OVER US FROM HEAVEN

On a Saturday afternoon in the winter of '79, my mother, Sister Michelle and I went to the Sears mall to spend some of my dad's hard earned money. I was a wide-eyed five-year-old kid who loved hanging out with my cool rock and roll mom and my sisters whom I always looked up to. The one thing I always remembered about Sears back in those days was all of the Winnie the Poo merchandise that hung on the walls and sat on the shelves. The store was always over saturated with Poo items. I was never into Winnie the Poo as a child but even to this day when I think of Winnie the Poo, I think of the Sears mall in Alaska. My sister went her separate way to look at the records and new releases. I stayed with my mother as she looked through the clothes on the racks.

I started to get a little bored and began playing hide and seek with my mom. I would hide behind the tall rack of clothes, and when my mom would say my name to find out where I was, I would jump out from behind the racks and make a monstrous sound to scare her. She would pretend that I scared her and jokingly say, "Don't ever scare me like that again." I would go back into hiding, and we would repeat this routine all over again.

I decided to make things more interesting and began running away from my mom through the tall racks of clothes. It was exciting blazing through all the clothes as they softly hit my face as I went through the maze like an adventurer. What would happen next or where I would end up I didn't know. All I knew at that time was I was the king of hide and seek, and nobody could find me unless I wanted them to.

A few minutes had gone by, and I went through the last of the clothing racks and found myself standing in the middle of the aisle. I looked to my left and then to my right, but my mother was nowhere to be seen. Instantly I was struck with the feeling of being all alone. At that moment, the ceiling and walls had become taller and wider. I spun in a circle frantically looking for my mom's face. I saw dozens of women, but none of them were my mom. I began crying, tears strolled down my face as I yelled out, "Momma momma" but she didn't hear me. Even other adults didn't bother to stop and help me. You see a little boy crying and yelling out for his mommy you'd think you would stop to help him. They just kept looking at me and walking by. I was all alone. Nobody was coming to help me. My beautiful mom whose face smiled at me every day was now gone, and I didn't know if I would ever see her again.

I stood in the middle of Sears sobbing, feeling left behind. Then, I heard a woman's voice speaking to me, "Anthony, come here." I looked up and saw a woman. She was glowing in a bright white light. I had never seen her before and didn't even question how she knew my name. Still, I did what I was told and walked over to her. The closer I got to her; I realized that she didn't have a lower body. I saw no visible body parts at all, just white energy that enveloped her. She looked mad and upset with me. She gave me a look of disapproval. She began to speak in a stern voice, "Anthony, why did you run away from your mother?" I just held my head down and sniffled, but I didn't answer her. A part of me understood that somehow, I knew this woman, and she knew me, but I didn't know how. I also knew that I would be safe and that I could trust her. "Come with me," she said and again in a stern voice.

I followed her through the mall, and she guided me to a bench and told me to sit down, I did what I was told. She looked down and spoke to me, "Anthony, you sit here and wait. A woman and her child will be along shortly to help you. Do not leave this bench!" Still sniffling, I nodded in grievance. Right in front of me, she disappeared.

I sat on that bench for what seemed like an eternity. I saw no sign of anyone coming to help me. I began to feel all alone and again started crying. Then, just like the lady in the bright light said, I was approached by a white woman with dark hair. She was pushing a shopping cart with a little boy inside of it. "What's wrong little girl," she said. At that age, I looked like a little girl with long hair and big puppy dog eyes. I looked up at her with tears running down my cheeks and said, "I can't find my mommy." "Oooh, don't cry sweetie, we'll find your mommy." She picked me up and hugged me as I cried on her shoulder. She put me in the shopping cart next to her little boy who seemed to be consumed with the big bag of popcorn he was eating.

We looked all over the mall for my mom, and I was like a hunting dog on patrol. Bless her heart, the nice lady kept pointing at black women asking if they were my mom. "No, that's not her," I would say. I think it was my thick uncombed hair that made her automatically assume that my mom would be black. After pointing at a dozen black women, I finally had to say to her, "My mom looks like you; her hair looks like yours." I think at that moment the lady got a clue that I was a mixed child. After about twenty more minutes of searching, I saw my mom come from around the corner. I shouted, "Mommy!" My mom approached us, and I put my arms out for a big hug. I was not letting go of her this time either. The woman said, "I found your daughter sitting on the bench crying because she said she couldn't find you. But I'm glad we did." My mom said humorously, "He's a boy, not a girl." They talked and laughed for a little bit. My mom told me to thank the nice lady, and we left.

Who was the stern mysterious spirit woman that helped me and was glowing with a bright white light around her? She was my grandmother, my mom's mother who had passed away years before. I know this because I would later recognize her from the pictures my mom would show me of her.

All this time, I thought that I had gathered Biblical knowledge, wisdom, insight and awareness so I could use what I've learned to help and assist others. When in fact, in the end, all I did was lord it over them.

4

GOD IS EVERYWHERE. EVEN WHEN YOU'RE CHASING FROGS

On a summer's afternoon in Anchorage, Alaska, my Brother Mark and I joined my dad at a construction site on the outskirts of the city where his company was working at. Mark was nine, and I was seven years old. We got bored listening to the men talking about the construction project and decided to break away to find some adventure. Mark and I wandered into a field. Some of the grass and branches were taller than we were and going inside didn't look safe at all. Also, some of the branches had very sharp edges. Because going into that field seemed like a bad idea, of course, Mark said, "Let's go in!"

Mark was grinning the whole time we were walking through the forbidden zone like he was waiting for something exciting to happen. I was just nervous and scared. Still, he was my big brother and if he would have said, "Let's run out into traffic wearing a blindfold," I probably would have done it. That's what little brothers do; they look up to and follow their big brothers off of cliffs.

As we got deeper into the field, we found ourselves in an area that was more open. Then, something jumped on my foot. It was a frog. Truth be told - I don't know the difference between a frog and a toad. I also don't know if they generally live in Alaska or if the property owner had put them there purposely to keep certain insects away. However, they were there.

Instantly our first instinct was to chase them, which is what we did. Mark was capturing them and putting them in his pockets. I wasn't fast enough, and they kept getting away from me. I tried my best but couldn't compete with my big brother who was catching these little Kermits with his athletic speed. Even as a kid, Mark was cool, fast and could run like the wind, qualities I would always be jealous of and wish I had while growing up. Instead, God gave me the leftovers in the DNA department, a chubby kid who looked like a girl with untamed hair.

I saw a frog on the ground; when I reached down to pick it up, it hopped away. I walked up to it and reached down again to pick it up, and again it hopped away. I don't know why I just didn't leave this little guy alone, but for some odd reason, I saw capturing this particular frog as a challenge. The frog was getting tired of me harassing it so it began to hop away from me as fast as it could. I wouldn't give up, and it turned into a Tom and Jerry chase. I was running out of breath, but I was still persistent, then the frog leaped through some tall bushes. I quickly went into the bushes after it. What I didn't know was that there was a creek on the other side of those bushes, and before I even knew what happened, I fell right into it.

I remember opening my eyes under water and was in an instant panic. The water was freezing and woke up every nerve in my body. The creek was at least thirteen feet deep, and the current was strong and pushing me downstream. I managed to get to the top and stick my head above water. I looked around hysterically to see what was happening and where I was at in the creek. As my head went in and out of the water, I managed to scream out Mark's name twice, but my big brother was nowhere to be found. Even as a little boy I knew that this was it for me. I saw no way out of this and nobody was around to help me. I was hysterical, crying, drowning and screaming at the same time. Only the sky above knew what was happening to me as I looked up to the clouds and cried. Then, something began to happen. Moreover, as long as I live I'll never forget seeing this. Unnaturally the water around me started making a whirlpool, and I felt my body was being pushed towards the creeks bank. I also realized that in the long stretch of bank that there was only one thick branch that was sticking out and I was being pushed into the direction of it. When I got close enough to the branch, I grabbed it for dear life and held onto it as tightly as I could.

The current was strong, and I could feel my hand losing its grip on the thick branch. I saw Mark running over to my rescue. Never was I so happy to see my big brother. I let go of the branch and grabbed his hand.

I could still feel my body being pulled from the rough water as Mark and the current played tug of war with me. Mark, though pulling as hard as he could was losing the battle and I could feel myself going deeper into the water. I knew my big brother couldn't hold me much longer, but then something happened. I saw a light shining behind Mark's back. This light behind him quickly began to grow. It got bigger and brighter. So bright, I could no longer see him; all I could see was this bright light shining in front of me. Even though it was illuminating bright it wasn't blinding, I could actually look directly into it without having to squint or blink. It was peaceful, beautiful. I was assured that everything would be ok and that the light was there to help us. I don't know if it was because I was so overwhelmed with the light, but I couldn't hear anything as well. The loud sound of the roaring creek, my brother's voice and the nature around us had just been silenced. All I knew at that moment was to stay focused on the light. When I was in the presence of the light, I no longer felt like a human. For that moment I felt like a spirit that understood the light, wisdom and His presence. I could feel the healing, endless love, and mercy in the bright light that went on forever.

I saw a man above me. He was surrounded by light. He was looking down at me and had a calm, peaceful smile, and love in his face. I couldn't see his hands, but I felt him grab my upper body and levitate my body out of the water and onto the bank. Then, the light disappeared, I could hear again and everything went back to normal.

Of course, I'm sure Mark thought he was the one who pulled me out of the ferocious creek. All he could say was "Look at your clothes, mom's gonna be mad at you."

I never told Mark about the bright light, the man or what I saw on that afternoon, but I'll always remember it.

I'm always amazed that doctors will charge thousands of
dollars to heal and operate just to save a human life.
Yet Jesus walked endless miles to heal and to
raise people from the dead for free.

5

THANK YOU FATHER FOR HEALING MY FINGER

It was October of 1986. My best friend Jimmy and I were outside riding our bikes and enjoying the pavement knowing that soon our Alaskan streets will be covered in snow and ice. We rode to our usual hangouts and after awhile ended up behind our junior high school. We liked racing our bikes on the school's track.

After a few laps, I noticed my back tire was a little wobbly. I got off and kneeled behind the back tire to investigate the problem. With the bike still standing, I jerked the back tire a little to see how loose it was. Then, I began to play with the chain to check the slack. My right-hand index finger was close to the sprocket and underneath the chain and I should have been more careful and paying attention. Before I knew what happened, the bike began moving forward, and my index finger went deep in between the chain and sprocket. It was so painful that I temporarily lost my vision for a few seconds. When my vision came back, I looked down, my finger was caught in between the chain and sprocket like a bear's paw caught in a trap, it was hideous. Dark purple blood was gushing out of it, and it looked like my finger had no more texture or meat in it. It looked like I had stuck it in a garbage disposal; just a mashed piece of tissue. Then, the bike fell to the ground, ripping more of my finger.

I screamed out to Jimmy, who came rushing to me. When he saw my finger lodged in between the bike chain and sprocket and the dark blood all over the ground he became temporarily grossed out, but he composed himself and told me to relax and not to move. He picked the bike up, with my finger still attached to the bike and me crying like a baby he said, "We're going to have to push the bike backward to get your finger out." I took a deep breath. "Ready?" he said, I nodded yes. Jimmy slowly pushed the bike backward and my finger was finally released. When I saw my finger, I could have just fainted right there. The only thing keeping my finger attached was a piece of skin. I cried even harder, knowing that I had just destroyed my finger, and it was going to have to come off.

While riding my bike home, I held my hand in the air with my finger dangling. All I could think about was showing it to my mother. While riding on the sidewalk, a man was walking in my direction, when he got close enough, he told me to stop. He was a tall red-haired man with a red mustache and was wearing an army jacket. Not knowing what this man wanted and still crying I yelled out, "What!" He looked at my hand concernedly and said, "It's going to be ok," and walked away. I had no idea what he was talking about or what he meant by telling me that "It's going to be ok?" However, I quickly forgot about him and kept riding home.

My mom rushed me to the hospital. When the doctor looked at my finger, he said, "I don't think I can save it. There is too much tear and damage. We are going to have to take it off." I cried some more, not only was I in pain but now it was official that I was going to lose my finger. My mom pleaded with the doctor to try anything he could to save my finger, but the doctor insisted that if he didn't take it off it could get infected and cause even more damage. After continuously jumping down his throat, he finally agreed not to take it off.

To this day, I don't even remember what the doctor did to my finger because while they were working on it, my mom kept telling me not to look at it and I didn't want to. However, it was finally bandaged up. The Doctor and my mother left the room for a moment to sign some paperwork. Shortly after, another doctor walked in. He said, "Hi Anthony, how are you?" He had a big smile and continued, "How's our tough guy today, is that hand feeling any better?" He was so full of energy that he didn't even give me the chance to answer the first question. I was in a sad state and kept my answers short. Then of all things he could have said to me, he asserted, "Do you always put that much grease in your hair, you must go through pillow cases like water?" Growing up, I always wore a lot of grease in my hair, nice of him to notice. Still, with his up-tempo attitude he made me smile and laugh a little. That's when I realized something, the weird doctor kind of looked liked the man that had stopped me on the sidewalk when I was riding my bike home. He was wearing a medical cap, but I could see some of the red hair sticking out and he had the same red mustache. I guess I thought it was just a coincidence that the sidewalk man and the doctor looked like the same person even with the same voice. Then, what happened next was even more strange behavior from the doctor. Though my hand was very sensitive and the first doctor stressed to me not to get it wet or put any pressure on it, this weird doctor grabbed my hand firmly and squeezed it hard. I let out a yell from the pain, he looked me in the eyes and said, "You won't feel any more pain, your finger will be healed." He released my hand, and I looked at him as if he were crazy. Then he left the room. Moments later, I realized that I didn't feel any more pain whatsoever from my finger or hand. The pain was totally gone.

When the first doctor came back into the room he asked me how I was feeling, I told him I was fine, and I had no more pain. I also told him about the other doctor who came in the room. He said there should have been no other doctor talking to me or looking at my hand. He asked what the other doctor looked like and when I described the weird doctor to him he said that no doctor or nurse on that particular staff fit that description, but he would look into it. He probably let it go after that.

Over the next month when I would get a finger cleaning and fresh bandages put on from my mom and school nurse I would never even look at my finger. I would turn the other way. They would both make comments about how it wasn't looking any better, but they tried to stay optimistic for my sake. After about four weeks of wearing this annoying bandage, I woke up one morning and realized that the bandage was completely off my finger and on the bed. I had no choice but to look at my finger. While looking at it, I was surprised and a little taken back. I thought to myself "That's weird, it looks perfectly fine and normal to me." It was as if it never happened. You couldn't even see where the chain cut through it. I wiggled it, applied pressure, even bit it but I felt nothing, and it was back to normal. I didn't understand what the school nurse or my mom, were talking about when they kept telling me how bad it was looking. When they both saw my brand new finger, they were in amazement and couldn't believe how nicely it healed up. Especially the school nurse. She was stunned that after all of the damage that was done to my finger that there wasn't even a scar, mark or anything as evidence that my finger was damaged or even cut in half.

I believe that the red-headed man on the sidewalk and the weird doctor were not only the same person but was an angel who had healed my finger. And he meant it when he said, "You won't feel any more pain, your finger will be healed."

Dear God. There's something about life that I don't understand and would like to talk to You about. Do You have an eternity to spare?

6

ONE LAST GOODBYE

In 1988, my Brother Mark had begun dating a girl named Tracie. They dated for a while and everything was going well until one night Tracie's life had come to an end. After driving home from a party on a cold November evening, her friend driving began to race the car next to theirs with Tracie in the passenger seat. After racing a few blocks, she lost control of the car and hit a brick wall. Tracie died instantly, and her friend died the next day at the hospital. For the next couple of days, Mark was very upset and crying uncontrollably. I, on the other hand, was very insensitive and was not being very supportive, so I left him alone. I didn't know how to console someone after a death. The only thing on my mind at that age was girls. But after that second night, I would be the one who would need consoling. On that evening, Mark had cried himself to sleep. I was cleaning my new pair of Adidas shoes and listening to N.W.A. on the headphones.

I kept hearing a loud noise at the window. It sounded like metal bending. I got up, walked to the window, and pulled the curtain back. I saw a girl. Normally our friends and girlfriends would come to our bedroom window so they didn't wake up our mom, but in this instance, I didn't recognize her. Still, she looked a little familiar. I also noticed that she had a strange greenish/red light around her body. The expression on her face was of one who was confused and lost, maybe on drugs. Then, I made another discovery; she had no lower body?

I also realized that the sound of metal bending was her hands pushing in the window forming two small bubbles. That's when I realized the impossible; I was making eye contact with my brother's dead girlfriend, Tracie. I ran out of the room as fast as I could and into my mom's room. I was freaked out and terrified. My mom asked me what was wrong, and I told her that Tracie was outside of our bedroom window, and I was serious.

My mom searched the bedroom and looked out the window but found nothing. I told her that Tracie was really outside the window, and I looked her in the eyes. I also told her that she was scared and seemed lost.

After I had calmed down a little, my mom explained to me that sometimes after people die, they don't crossover right away and sometimes they'll just linger around for awhile and visit family and familiar places. They're not ready to leave their loved ones just yet which was why Tracie was there. She came to visit my brother, but I was the one who found her instead. In retrospect, my mom's explanation sounded good, but at that time all I heard was, "Blah, blah, blah, and blah."

All I knew was there was a girl outside of my bedroom window who was supposed to be dead. So for the next six months, I wouldn't stay in the house by myself. If nobody was home after school, I would go to the 7-11 across the street and play video games until someone came home. I wouldn't sleep in that room anymore. I would sleep on the couch. If I needed clothes, I would go in there and grab what I needed and hurry out. I didn't mean any disrespect towards Tracie; I was just a scared fourteen-year-old.

I pray Tracie has passed on to the other side peacefully.

PREMONITIONS

In this day and age in the American culture, the word 'psychic' has been muddled and conflicted to the point of misconception. Because of that, I would never consider myself psychic but spiritually sensitive.

It was around the age of eleven and twelve when I began to see bright lights that would outline the outside of people's bodies. Sometimes the lights that would radiate from them would be green or orange, but most of the time it would just be white. This continued throughout my adulthood. In my mid-twenties, I was told that the bright lights I was seeing around people were really their auras, and some people could see them and some couldn't. I could also see dark outlines around people's bodies. Sometimes it would almost look like smoke. I was told that these were people who were spiritually negative and this dark negative energy emerged from them.

I would also spontaneously have premonitions about things that would happen in the near future or visions of something that happened in the past, especially death. So many times, for no reason at all, if it were someone I knew whether it was a co-worker, associate, family member or friend of a friend, I would know of their coming death! I could be hanging out, watching T.V. or just driving and the face of someone I knew would appear in my mind clear and sharp. Right then I would know that they were going to die soon! That person would usually die within a week or two from my premonition. I have had instances where I would run into a friend I haven't seen in a long time, and we would start talking, and I would get an image in my mind that someone we both know is dead. When I would ask them, they would validate me.

I could also pick up and feel the energy in a room or an environment. As a young teen, while hanging out with my friends, we would sometimes walk into a room or building, and I would automatically feel the negative ambiance. I would ask my friends if they could feel the negative energy like something dreadful has happened there. Of course, they didn't know what I was talking about and how could they because I barely understood what was happening myself. All I knew was that I could feel the pain from a past moment in that room. There have been times where I have walked into rooms and have been overwhelmed with a sad feeling. I would almost want to break down and cry. It was like I was absorbing the residue of a past tragic incident that took place in that room. My friends would ask me what was wrong, and I would just say I was tired.

As an adult, I would walk into churches and automatically know if there were negative spirits inside of it. There would be a thickness in the atmosphere. I would always feel like I was suffocating and the ceiling and walls were closing in on me. I would see dark figures quickly moving around the room and wondering if anybody else was seeing this too. In one church I attended, I remember staring at the preacher on stage. He had an aura of darkness that radiated from his body and on both sides of him stood two dark figures posted like guards. I suppose they were trying to protect their investment so to speak.

I could also pick up and feel the energy from a still picture. For a long time, I couldn't understand why I would get emotional looking at certain pictures, but I could definitely feel the pain from the individuals in the photos. I would later read how people who were spiritually sensitive could get energy and information just from holding or concentrating on photos or clothing.

I could also recollect things that happened to me as a baby. I told my mom how we would go sledding on the hill in the back of our apartment building. I told her I was wearing a light blue snowsuit. She had on a red jacket and snow cap; the sled was yellow, and the hill pointed north. She told me I was only five months old when we would do that. I would also go into details about other things that happened before I was a year old and she would get a kick out of it.

There were also some funny moments like as an adult while at work; I was talking to a customer and in my mind, I knew she had lived in Africa.

During our conversation, I asked her, "So what was it like living in Africa?" She looked at me stunned and said, "How did you know I lived in Africa?" I felt pretty stupid because I didn't have an answer, so all I could say was, "Lucky guess."

One day my best friend Jimmy and I were at the local college watching the talent show. The MC said they were giving away prizes, and they were going to call out three seat numbers. If they called your seat number, you won a prize. Before the MC announced the winning numbers, I told Jimmy what they were going to be, and I was right. For the longest time, Jimmy wouldn't shut up about it and would always nag me about how I knew what the numbers were going to be.

As we got older, Jimmy would become a spectator to a lot of my premonitions. He would always ask questions about it and say things like, "We should go to Vegas and gamble" or "I'm gonna have my sister in the states buy us lottery tickets, and you guess what the numbers will be, and we'll split the money 50/50." I would laugh, but he was dead serious.

It wasn't something I could control. I know there are individuals who are gifted in those areas and could manage it, but I wasn't one of them. There are ways to exercise and strengthen your abilities, but I never cared to do any of those things.

Whenever I would have premonitions or insight of any kind, it was always spontaneous and involuntary, and I prefer it that way. As a teenager, I tried to suppress and ignore it thinking it would eventually go away, but it didn't. As I got older and the stress and worries of life began to occupy my mind, the premonitions became less and less, but still, they continue.

This following chapter is an example of how having the ability to see future events isn't always a positive thing; especially when it concerns loved ones and friends.

Hello Satan, it's me. I got your message that you wanted to get together again. On Sundays, I'm usually at God's house, but I'm available the rest of the week. Call me back and let me know.

7

DARK APARTMENT

At sixteen, I was working at one of the popular pizza franchises of the time. It was a dead end job that was dirty and at the end of the day, I would reek of bad food.

No matter how much I showered and scrubbed, that pizza smell wouldn't come off of me, but I did what I had to do. I had already dropped out of school because I just didn't like it. I had no motivation for school. I never studied for tests. I never did homework, and it seemed like an inconvenience and a waste of a day.

One afternoon while I was working, my best friend Jimmy came by to see me. He had brought our friend George with him. George was a couple of years older than us and was a part of the clique that included Jimmy's older brother and my Brother Mark.

I came out of the kitchen to greet them and after slapping hands and fist pounds, Jimmy said, "When you get a second, come sit with us. George wants to talk to you about something." I gave them plates and soda cups for the buffet, and said, "Give me fifteen minutes." During those fifteen minutes, I wondered what George would want to talk to me about. George was a successful drug dealer who had girls, nice cars, and at least three different condo apartments, so what was his interest in me?

I went on a break and sat down with them ready to hear something interesting. George spoke up, "Anthony I wanna offer you a job. I know you're not happy tossing pizza dough in the air every day, so I'm gonna give you a chance to make some real money. Jimmy's already vouched for you and says you can be trusted. I believe him."

As George continued talking, I started to get tense because I knew this was about selling crack cocaine and that concept was different and taboo for me. I had no problem with being a car thief or breaking into people's homes, but crack was something else!

In the late 80's and early 90's, it was relatively easy to sell drugs in Alaska because there wasn't a lot of heat or pressure from the cops or F.B.I. They just weren't ready for the epidemic of this thing called crack cocaine that would sweep the city during that era. The two neighborhoods in Anchorage that held the majority clientele were Mountain View and Fairview. You couldn't even drive through these neighborhoods without some dope addict throwing his hands up in the air at you. That signal meant "do you have any drugs?"

A lot of guys I grew up with during that era gave up school and sports to sell drugs because the money was just too fast and easy. These days, it's hard and next to impossible to be a successful drug dealer in Alaska. The federal agents are too smart, and they give out twenty-five to forty year sentences like candy. I guess all things must change!

Between both neighborhoods, George had up to six spots, meaning six different apartments where drugs were sold. All of them did well, but there was one spot specifically in the neighborhood of Fairview that was a real money maker. George told me that because there was so much money going through there, he didn't think his workers could handle it, and he thought they were stealing. He told me he wanted me to work there, and he would teach me everything I needed to know.

Besides trusting me, I believe another reason George chose me was because I knew the streets, hung out in the streets and had friends from the streets, but I didn't have a street mentality. I also felt that he wasn't just asking me to work for him, but he was also asking for a favor. I didn't mind doing George a favor and I would get paid well for it. Even as a young kid, I always liked and respected George. He was always cool to me and would say, "Anthony, if anybody gives you a hard time or fucks with you, let me know." I really didn't have to think about it. I accepted his offer.

My official job as a crack dealer began the next day. I was working twelve hours a day from night until morning. The job was effortless. All I had to do was watch T.V., play video games, and sleep. Whenever someone knocked on the door, I would go into the bedroom and the owner of the apartment, Bob, dealt with the business transaction as a middle man. Bob would bring me the money and I would give Bob the product. The job was that easy. In return for letting George use their homes for drug traffic, George would pay their rent, their utilities, and give them extra money and dope. Being that they were poor and addicts, this was an offer they couldn't refuse.

I didn't trust Bob. At all times, I had wads of cash in all my pockets plus product, and Bob was such an addict, I didn't know if he was going to crack one day and try to rob me. Some nights it wasn't easy working there because Bob would get really high and then start tweaking really bad and get aggressive. One night, I got in his face and cussed him out. I thought I had put him in his place; I was wrong. The next night, he tried to have me set up. There was a knock at the door, so I went into the bedroom. As usual, I peeked through the door and saw Bob let two guys in. I heard Bob say to them, "He's in the bedroom. Hurry up and make sure you get all the money." One of the men pulled a gun out of his jacket and had a look in his eyes like he would kill for twenty dollars! I ran to the window and struggled to get through it, but when I finally got out, I fell three stories to the ground. I got up and limped away as fast as I could. George went over there the next day and Bob wasn't there and never seen again.

After working at a few more spots, over a period of time, I earned George's trust and confidence. My money was never short. I was always on time, always showed up for work, and I never tried to bullshit George. I was always upfront. I was so punctual that you would have thought I was working undercover for the cops, but the truth was, I was making more money than I had ever made and I wasn't about to blow it.

One day George said he was going to take me out of the spots, meaning out of the dope houses and put me on the streets to be a runner. I was happy about that. It was the equivalent of a meter maid being promoted to detective. He gave me a beeper. My new job was to wait for it to go off and make deliveries. Some of the customers were ok, while others you had to be on guard. An example: the time I went to a ladies house. She answered the door wearing panties and a bathrobe. Her breasts were hanging out. She said, "I don't have any money, but I'll fuck you for a half." That meant $50.00 worth of product. "If you ain't got no money, I'm leaving," I said. "Ok, I'll suck your dick for a quarter piece" she replied. When I rejected her again, she started crying and begging, "Please, I really need it. Come on. What do you want me to do? I told you we could fuck. Please, just a quarter piece." It was sad. I just walked away.

Another time, I went to a trailer park and a skinny white guy opened the door completely naked. He also had a gun in his hand. I refused to enter the trailer and said in a tough voice, "Man, give me the money so I can get the fuck out of here." He pointed his gun at me and said, "You know what's wrong with the world today? Niggers. You people make the world a horrible place." Then he started laughing. "I'm joking with you. Here's your money. You wanna come in and have a drink?" I turned the drink down and left.

One night, I went to make a sale in the neighborhood of Mountain View. When I arrived at the house, another dealer named Rodrick was there. The man said he wanted to buy a half but he wanted to see who had the bigger half. I pulled my biggest half piece out, and Rodrick clearly saw that he couldn't compete pulled out his gun and put it to my head. Pushing the tip of the barrel into my skull, he said, "Hey nigga, peep this. You tell George to stay the fuck out of Mountain View. If I catch you niggas over here again, it's gonna be on." I could smell the liquor on his breath and the weed on his clothes, but to save face I challenged him, I said, "Hey nigga, why you hidin' behind a gun and your boys? We can go outside right now." His partner punched me in the face then also pulled his gun on me. They were so intoxicated that if I had swung back, I would be dead right now. Afterward, I walked to the nearest payphone and called George. He rounded up a little posse and went looking for Rodrick and his boys. When he finally caught up with him, the result was Rodrick ended up working for George anyway. A few years ago, I heard that Rodrick was serving a life sentence for shooting his girlfriend in the head for talking back to him.

I began having close calls with the law. One time was when George sent me out to the small town of Wasilla, home of Sarah Palin, to buy a grocery bag full of marijuana. It was so intense that my whole car smelled of it, and I had to keep all of the windows rolled down. Only a few blocks away from my drop off, I ran a yellow light and a cop pulled me over.

I was sweating bullets. The whole car was reeking of marijuana and even if the officer had a bad cold, he would still have to smell it. He told me why he pulled me over and asked for my license. I was carrying my Brother

Mark's license and that's what I gave him, he said he'd be right back. I sat there for a half hour. "What was he doing? Was he waiting for backup? Did he smell the weed and call for a police dog?" A million thoughts raced through my mind! He opened his door. I put the car in drive. If he said, "Please step out of the car," I was going to punch it.

At this point, I was high on the marijuana residue and ready for anything. He said, "Mark, I'm giving you a ticket for running a red light. Please sign here." I didn't even try to argue that the light was yellow. I signed the document and he let me go.

One morning, my mom woke me up and said, "There're three F.B.I agents at the door, and they wanna talk to you." Not a pleasant way to wake up. When I saw the agents, they looked like something out of a movie; wearing black trench jackets and mirrored black shoes. They took me to the laundry room of my building to ask me some questions. I thought the jig was up and my dirty deeds had finally caught up with me. They presented a federal photo album full of men that were wanted and being watched. At least, that's what I assumed it was. "We know who you are Anthony. Now we want to ask you some questions." They asked me a lot of questions and of course, I said "No" to everything. They showed me some pictures from the album and asked if I knew who certain drug dealers and criminals were. Again, I said I didn't know or recognize the individuals in the photos. "Ok thank you for your time," and just like that they left. I believed it to be some kind of a setup, but of what I didn't know, so I watched my back a little closer.

Shortly after, George rented a new spot in Fairview to bring traffic through. Spots in Fairview didn't last long because the police would eventually get wise and locations would have to be changed every few months. George picked me up and took me to the new location. When I walked into the apartment, immediately, I was overwhelmed with death and pain. Right then and there, I knew something bad was going to happen in that apartment. It was too much; I started getting dizzy. I was having a premonition of death in that very apartment. And it would be soon. But of whom I didn't know. I knew it could easily be me! Or even George. I went outside for air. I knew I had to tell George we have to let this apartment go and find another spot. I couldn't come out and say, "Hey, George, I have psychic premonitions and I feel that soon death will happen here in this apartment, so let's forget all about it and go get ice cream." So I made up a lie about knowing some other dealers who got busted in the building next door. George replied that we'd just have to be more careful. I wasn't going to stress about it that day, but I knew I would have to keep working on him to stay away from that apartment. In the meantime, I had a plan and an idea of taking over the whole city and monopolizing the crack scene altogether.

I worked on my plan for a month and was waiting for the opportune time to present it to George. Again, George was already a successful drug dealer, but I still saw a lot of room for improvement. The advantages I had over a lot of dealers were that I was very organized and I knew how to analyze situations, I wasn't greedy, and I didn't think with my ego. Over a period of time, I've watched the behaviors of the other dope dealers and they were all self-destructive. The idea in the game was to make as much money as you could and stay low key. But these guys wanted reputations and to be known as drug dealers. They drove expensive flashy cars with loud music pushing out heavy bass! They would make deals right in the open in the middle of the streets. They also liked to impress girls, so they would let their air-head immature girlfriends know all of their business. They might as well have been walking down the street and carrying signs that said, "I'M A DRUG DEALER." Plus, they also treated their customers like shit, which didn't make a lot of sense to me. If someone has money to give you, you give them customer service with a smile, even if it was an addict! It was only a matter of time until they all got popped and most of them did and are still serving long sentences.

I wanted to create an organization that was a convenient store/ McDonald's of the Alaska drug world. With George as the head and my best friend Jimmy and I would run the operation and have carefully watched workers under us. Like any professional business, we would have meetings twice a week and pay our employees double what they were already making.

The main focus was the customer's happiness always comes first. Our gimmick would be that we would reduce everything. Instead of paying $50.00 for a half, you'll only pay $25.00 and still get twice the product. That would be for quarters, halves and grams and so on. Initially, that would sound crazy, but I would have to convince George that we would monopolize the entire market this way. It was simple. We would also deliver any hour of the night within thirty minutes with a smile. The psychology was easy. If people we're going to give you money, try to create ways to please them even more. A lot of dealers would get paged and make their customers wait for over two hours for them. That didn't make sense to me. If someone's got your money - you go and get it. Also, we would figure out the names and the schedules of police officers in the neighborhoods and hire people to specifically listen to police scanners on eight-hour shifts. I can't go too deep into the entire layout without sounding like an active criminal, but that was the minor of it.

One night, I decided that I would approach George about my plan the following day. I was sure he'd go for it because he trusted my opinion and he knew I had a good mind for organization and planning. That night I went to sleep full of confidence.

The next morning I woke up to my phone ringing, it was Jimmy. His voice was soft as he spoke,

"Anthony, where have you been all night?"

"I been right here," I responded.

"You don't know then."

"Know what?" I asked.

"Someone killed George!"

After taking a few minutes to gather my emotions, we spent the next hour talking about George's murder, both of us still in shock. George was shot twice in the chest, and his friend who was with him was shot once in the head and once in the stomach, in that very apartment, where I had the deathly premonition. The lead detective said George's eyes and mouth were open, and his facial expression looked as if he were saying, "why?" It was later discovered after arrests were made that the murderers were crack heads. After I had hung up with Jimmy, all I could do was stare at the wall and cry. George was murdered. I couldn't believe it. Instead of working on my plan to take over the city, I should have been working on George to stay away from that apartment. He might still be alive today. I collected all of the drugs I had in my possession and flushed all of it down the toilet. I never participated in criminal activity again.

Why do I ask you how you feel when I don't care? Why do I ask you what's on your mind when I don't want to hear it? Why do I ask you if you need help when I don't want to help you? Why do I show concern when I have none. I don't know? Just make sure you're there for me when I need you.

8

IF GOD WOULD BRING A FLY BACK TO LIFE, HOW MUCH MORE VALUABLE ARE YOU?

I was at home one afternoon, sitting on the recliner, sad and reading my Bible. I guess I wouldn't say reading my Bible as much as looking at the words on the page and trying to stay focused and make sense of what I was reading. The past two weeks prior I had been hurting, suffering and trying to work through some personal issues I was dealing with and as a result, I had slipped into a bad depression; a dreadful depression. I was in a mindset of hopelessness, and even though the afternoon sun that was shining outside was brighter than it had been in a long time, my eyes only saw darkness. I felt like I really needed help, some form of spiritual attention, so I did what my Sister Lorraine told me to do whenever I felt I was at a low point in my life which at that time seemed to be all the time "Read my Bible!"

The reason I didn't want to read my Bible was that usually when I'm depressed I'll have a very low attention span and reading a Bible that made no sense to me at the time was really the last thing I wanted to be doing. I was at a low point in my life, but also it was at a time when I was trying to get to know God, His ways and the Word, and do it through my suffering. Still, I hadn't had a relationship with Him. Also, I had an emptiness inside of me that I knew somehow only God could feel, but where the hell was He? Also, why would He help me? At this time the church and Bible stuff was new to me.

I didn't have a church home; I had been attending my sister's church as a guest. I wasn't like all those other Christians who went there that were loyal in heart and attendance. Those followers had a major head start on me. They knew their Bibles well. They knew all the words to the songs that were sung in the church and how to cry out with real tears as they sang these songs. They knew how to converse and to relate to other followers about the things of God and scripture. They knew how to be vulnerable and weren't ashamed to show weakness with one another. They went to every social event and meetings the church would schedule. They participated in the church's outreach programs and went to the prison, hospitals, and homeless shelters; they walked the streets and gave thousands of people who were suffering and in need of prayer hope. Last, but not least, they went to this church because they wanted to be there, not just because they were hurting or going through some crisis in their lives. I didn't fit any of the above criteria. I knew who I was on the inside, and I was anything but wanting to be spiritual. Nor did I want to truly have a personal relationship with God.

For a guy who deep down really didn't care about being a Christian and really didn't want to be there but had to be there to get some help or answers I needed at the time, I have to admit that I was extremely jealous of their commitment and relationship that they had with God. They wanted to love God and praise His name for who He was, not for what they could get from Him. It was impressive. I was only there for what I could get from Him. I remember feeling like whether I wanted to be there or not, they were going to move forward in their spiritual growth and maturity and succeed in doing so. The choice was mine to put forth the effort, and I chose not to. So at the time I decided to play the church role of user and taker. "I'll take what I need from the church and its members but beyond that, you probably won't be seeing that much of me, but if I'm in need of help or sympathy, I'll expect everyone to be there and pity me."

On this particular afternoon at home, I really needed help and sympathy, and because I chose to be a selfish man I found myself alone. I was in a position where I had no man or woman to cry out to. All I had was my depression and God to cry out to. Still sitting in the chair, I closed my Bible and placed it on the floor beside me. I just stared at the wall for about twenty minutes. After awhile my eyes began to fill with tears as I grieved. Nobody saw me crying, and nobody cared. Nobody was calling or knocking at my door. In my mind, I was in a lonely isolated place. To the right of me was an end table. On this end table was a small puddle of spilled water, in the water was a dead fly that had been lying on its side on the table for at least three days. I remember thinking that it was odd for that dead fly to still be there because my mother was such a neat freak. She was always constantly cleaning and scrubbing the house, so for her to let this dead fly lay there for three days and not pick it up was not like her at all and strange to me. I knew these past few days that the dead fly was there on the table, but being the lazy guy that I was when it came to housekeeping I chose to ignore it and wait for my mother to notice it and clean it up. Besides, dead carcasses freak me out, whether it's human, dog, or just a fly. My mind has always had a hard time comprehending how something once had life in it than all of a sudden it's a dead piece of flesh, so that made it too weird for me to touch. I just stared at the fly. For a moment it took my mind off my problems as I wondered how it died on that spot on the table. I wondered, "How come when a dog or cat dies we as people become sad to see a large animal hurting or killed, but when a bee or fly dies they're just small disposable creatures to us. Still, God created this little creature and gave it life just like He did for me." Then, at that very moment, something began to come over me.

I didn't know what was coming over me, but something was beginning to happen. At that very moment, I felt compelled to do something bold, not just for someone else but for a common house fly. I felt an energy and excitement go through my body like never before. What I was thinking about doing was outrageous, but I wanted to do it. I felt God was putting this on my heart to do this. It was almost as if God were saying to me, "Just try it and don't be afraid to ask Me, I'll show you what I can do in your life." At that moment I felt that God wanted to reveal Himself to me more personally and to make His presence in my life more real to me. He was showing me that I wasn't only doing this for the fly but for myself. I needed to do this for my spirit.

I got out of my chair and kneeled down in front of the end table. Staring at the dead fly, I began to speak to God out loud and said exactly what was in my heart. To this day I still remember the exact words I said to Him, "God, I'm hurting right now, I'm hurting really bad. I just need to know that You know what I'm going through, and You're there."

Somehow I knew that God was there. I felt a presence in the small living room - Energy. I continued, "If You would just give me some sort of sign to let me know that You care about me and You know what I'm going through it would help me get through this because I'll know You're with me." Then that big moment came when I had to be bold and ask God to do what most people and even the most devoted Christian would consider to be the unthinkable to do. But I was desperate, and I needed an in your face answer now, not tomorrow or a month from today, I needed to know God loved and wanted to help even a person like me who was usually full of shit. When you're at a low point in your life where you feel you're at your weakest, and you just don't care anymore and have nothing else to lose, like a homeless man on the street you'll ask for anything and won't care who's looking or even if you get rejected. I just knew at that moment I needed something big to happen, to know that God really knew me and that I wasn't just here on earth or in Alaska existing without purpose or meaning and that even my suffering had a purpose. I continued with deep sincerity, "God I know that this fly is small and insignificant to You, but still, it is one of Your creatures that You once gave life to. Will You please show me that You love me by bringing this little bug back to life, please God. Just give me a sign that You understand the pain that I'm going through. Amen." I had done it. I had asked God to bring a dead creature back to life. I asked God to let this creature breathe and live once again.

After I had prayed, I continued to sit on my knees, fixated on the fly. I was anxious because I wanted God to show me and give me the sign that I had asked for. Deep down I was expecting it to happen, but I also knew that I didn't have a personal relationship with God, so who was I to even ask for the crumbs that fell off of the master's table? Two minutes had passed. Still, nothing happened, I began to doubt. More time had passed, and my doubt increased. The lifeless fly just laid there motionless. After awhile I came to the conclusion that God really didn't know, hear or even care about me. I got up, sat back in the chair, closed my eyes and just cried. Tears rolled down my face, and I was back to being consumed with hopelessness, feeling forsaken and thoughts of abandonment.

About ten more minutes had passed, and the house was silent except for the sounds of my sniffling nose. "Maybe I should turn the TV on for some noise," I thought. At that moment I slowly turned to my right to look at the fly again to humor myself, I was in for the shock of a lifetime by what I would see next. The fly, still lying on its side was moving its left wing. I stared in amazement. It was actually moving its wing? It did this for about fifteen seconds. Then it stood up on its legs, I couldn't believe it. My heart continued to race as I watched the fly rubbing its two front legs together in a fast motion. The fly moved around for awhile as if adjusting itself, it was like an airplane warming up its engine and making sure everything was working properly. Then the right wing began moving, I was so stunned I couldn't even blink. A few seconds later the fly leaped into the air like it knew it had a new lease on life. It flew around the living room like it was the happiest fly in the world. Then something even more amazing happened, the fly actually flew in front of my face and stayed there for a moment, almost as if it were saying to me, "thank you." Then after flying around in a circle in the living room for a few minutes, it flew out of the open window. All I could do was stare in amazement!

God didn't bring this little fly back to life just to give me a sign. He was trying to show me that just as the fly, He could bring my heart, mind and spirit back to life and also give me a new lease on life. But all I had to do was come to Him. He was also letting me know that the hairs on my head are numbered, and a sparrow won't fall out of the sky without Him knowing about it. He had known me before I was in my mother's womb, and everything I do in my life that is good, loving, helpful, sincere, evil, ugly, hurtful, and unjust, or during my time of need and when I cry out to Him, He knows about it. He hears me, He watches me, He sees me, He walks with me, and last but not least, He knows me!

Once Satan approached me in the house of the Lord and said, "You're a phony,
a fraud, insincere and a weak coward who is scared of his own shadow!"
I replied, "Thank you, thank you, thank you for exposing me, I
didn't know how much longer I could keep up this masquerade."

9

THE GOLDEN MAN

One evening in the winter of 1994, I found myself wandering a shopping mall looking for a shirt to go with the slacks I had recently purchased and I couldn't find anything I liked. I guess I wouldn't say I was shopping as much as I was trying to keep my mind off of my depression and what was bothering me, so going to the mall and spending some money was an excuse and a way of getting out of the house. There are times when you want to get out of the house and spend time with friends, and then there are times when you want to get out of the house and just be by yourself. This was one of those; "Everybody leave me the hell alone!" days.

The mall was brightly lit, and it was packed with shoppers for the holiday season. You couldn't have walked five feet without having to say "excuse me" to somebody. Holiday music was playing through the intercoms, tall Christmas trees were set up everywhere throughout the mall, different colored ornaments were hung beautifully on the ceilings and walls. Something about the holidays can bring out the best in people or the worst in people, on this particular month it was bringing out the worst in me.

It's funny how you can be in an environment where there's a lot of people but still feel alone and by yourself. I began to realize that my attempt to get my mind off of what was bothering me, or should I say emotionally bringing me down was pointless. I found myself just roaming the mall and looking intently at items I knew I had no interest in purchasing. Also doing my best to avoid people and associates I knew, because of the way

I was feeling the last thing I wanted to do was make small talk or force conversation.

I felt it was time to go home. If I was going to continue to feel depressed and down, at least I could be in the comfort of my own couch and keep myself entertained by the idiot box. As I was making my way out of the mall I heard God speak to me; He said, "Go to your sister's church." The last thing I wanted to do that evening was to go to a church. Only because it would mean that I would have to interact in conversation with the members there and that was the last thing I wanted to do. Again I wanted to be left alone. I know now when I'm feeling low that church and being around fellow members is the place I need to be at, but at this time I still had a lot to learn. I replied back to God in my mind and said, "I'm not going to my sister's church; I don't want to be there tonight."

I left the mall, and as I drove into the winter night, God kept working on me. "Go to your sister's church," I heard Him say again. I kept trying to ignore His order while I cautiously drove on the icy roads, but I had to admit to myself that the impression He was given me was strong. I spoke out loud to God and said, "It's not that I don't want to actually go there, it's just that I feel too emotionally weak to even walk in the front door." God replied back again "Go to your sister's church." After awhile I found myself still fighting but beginning to give in because the message was so pertinent that God might as well have been sitting in my passenger seat. Now I was mad at Him. He was going to make me do something I didn't want to do and be somewhere that I didn't want to be. Or maybe that was just an excuse and God wasn't making me do anything against my will, perhaps I was just actually curious to see what He had in mind and why He was trying to lead me there. So I went to my sister's church. In my mind, I was kicking and screaming all the way there, but at the same time, I was kind of glad that I was being pulled.

I just sat in the parking lot of the church, staring at the white building. Everything inside of me did not want to step one foot into that building, but God was saying that this is what He wanted me to do. If I were angry at God, I would have just said no and went home, but on this evening I was just sad and depressed. I could already hear the spiritual party happening inside as I grabbed the handle to the front door. I entered the church, luckily there was no fanfare for me, and maybe three people turned around to see who had come through the door. I sat in the back so as not to be seen and also so I could quickly and easily sneak out the door when it was over. The pastor continued on with the Thursday night Bible study. His inspiring words shot out of his mouth like lightning; he spoke with conviction and power. Both men and women were being spiritually filled as they waved their hands back and forth in the air in approval. The pastor had the hookup, and everybody there wanted to buy the spiritual drugs directly from his dealer. Whatever problems these members walked in with were left at the bottom of their feet as they were being uplifted, and as they shouted out accolades to the pastor, "Teach it! C'mon pastor! Sure you right! Amen!" You could feel the Holy Spirit in the room, and everybody was getting in on the action; everybody except me.

I continued to just sit there in the back of the church feeling like I had a ton of bricks weighing me down. I had just heard some of the most awesome and inspiring words that had brought so much energy into the room from the pastor, but yet it went into one ear and out the other. In my head, the lights were on, but nobody was home. "God, why did you bring me here? What's this all about? Did God say something to me through the pastor and I missed His message?" I wondered. "Am I being so self-indulged in my sorrows that the meaning had passed me by? Or did I just waste my time when I could have kept driving home and still felt the same way." I thought to myself.

The choir went on stage in their street clothes to sing a song and bring the Bible study and night to an end. The song was beautiful, almost tear moving. At least to everybody else in the room who was singing along? To me, it was just time-consuming. Finally, it was all over. Everybody stood up to prepare to leave. "Was this it?" I wondered. "Should I just stay a little bit longer to see if something might happen?" I really didn't want me coming there to be one big waste of time, so I decided to just wait a few more minutes and grabbed the Bible off the chair ahead of me and pretended to read it.

Some of the members inside were still talking and laughing amongst themselves, some were getting their kids ready to leave, some were lined up to talk to the pastor, and some approached me to give me a hug or just to shake my hand as they exited the building. I put on a fake smile and small talk performance and tried to match their positive energy. But I'm sure those who spoke to me knew something was wrong. No matter how big your smile is, the eyes never lie.

By now most of the church was empty, and the only people that remained were the handful waiting to talk to the pastor. I decided that was it. "Nothing special was going to happen. I wasted my time coming here, and maybe I had fooled myself into thinking that God was speaking to me. Still the impression was so strong, how could I have been wrong about hearing His voice, I knew God had told me to come here." Not only was I feeling low, but now I had felt misled. I gathered what was left of my pity and headed for the door.

I took about four steps when I felt a hand grab my right shoulder, and I heard a voice, "Brother how are you doing tonight?" I turned around and saw a tall, dark skinned brotha looking down on me. He had the biggest smile I had ever seen. "Let me talk to you for a moment," he said. Now putting his hand on my left shoulder, he continued to smile at me and said, "Do you know how much God loves you, Anthony." I didn't question how he even knew my name. "Every day of your life God has put His angels around you to protect you and watch over you. The devil has a contract out on you with a price so big that demons are working overtime in trying to destroy you to collect on it. The devil doesn't put a big price on just anybody's head, only those he considers being a threat to him. He knows the favor you have with God and that God placed you on the earth for a specific reason. The devil knows what God has put inside of you even if you don't. The devil is scared of you and is doing everything in his power to make sure what the Father has put inside of you never comes out. This is why you suffer from depression, darkness, and hopelessness, because the demons are working on you night and day, I know you've seen them with your own eyes. The devil is frustrated because he wants you, but he can't have you and he's never going to give up on trying to destroy you."

As he spoke I felt his magnetism, he had an energy that was radiating off of his body and it was drawing my energy to him. Every word he spoke had power behind it, and I felt it. But what really kept me in awe was he had a bright golden light that was glowing around his body. That golden light was bright and endless. In that bright golden light I could see wisdom, peace, understanding, and last but not least, a bigger plan for my life and a world that went far beyond my issues or problems. Yes, instantly I knew he wasn't of this earth. My spirit knows when an angel or spiritual being is talking to me, and I also knew when to just listen, which is what I did.

"The Father hears you when you pray and talk to Him. He's not ignoring you, Anthony. He knows what your problems are and what you deal with daily. He knows everything years in advance that's going to happen to you before you do. You will come out shining on the other side. Everything you go through is a part of His plan to benefit you, not to hurt you. He is so in love with you, and He has you right where He wants you, Anthony, He has you. You're His son, and the Father always protects His children."

When he was done speaking the man gave me a hug, then smiled at me and said, "I'll see you again soon." He walked out of the front door. I sat down on one of the chairs smiling and reflecting on his words. I felt new again, knowing that I had just received a spiritual reminder of my "importance." Whatever it is to this day I still don't know? But I felt good again, emotionally and spiritually reborn. I gathered my composure and headed for the door. As I opened the front door to the church, I saw it had begun to snow. When I looked down at the walkway, I saw that there were no footprints where his should have been?

10

ANGELS IN THE ODDEST PLACES

One evening I went to an adult bookstore on the other side of town. I wanted to see what they had in there and if their items were different than the adult bookstore where I usually frequented once a month to get my two favorite reading materials, Black Tail and Brown Sugar magazines. As I walked in the store the first thing I noticed was that it was very small. It didn't have much in there, but I will say that it was cleaner and smelled better than the adult bookstore I usually went to in downtown Anchorage. Obviously a waste of gas and time, but, I decided that since I was there, I would take a look around. Though I never bought sex toys, I laughed to myself at some of the items they had such as vibrators that were so big that they looked like they would put any woman in the hospital if she dared used them. As much as I was weirded out by some of the stuff that they had in the store, I still couldn't look away. It was too funny.

As I continued my tour, my eyes were drawn to a man who was standing in the cornered area of the store. He was standing in the area where they sell the gay magazines and items. He was calmly flipping through a magazine, but I could also see that he was checking me out. He was trying to look casual and nonchalant. He tried to act like he was in his own world and oblivious to what was going on around him, but I know that behavior when someone's checking me out because it's the same type of behavior I display when I'm trying to check out a woman in public. His eyes, body language, and demeanor were saying, "Ooh, that guy's hot, what a nice piece of ass." I was such a conceited guy at the time I guessed I assumed whether man or woman everybody was checking me out and looked at me as being a sexy hot piece of ass. Well, this ass says exit only, and nothing is going up in there unless I get abducted by aliens and that would be the only exception.

I continued looking around the store, and as the minutes went by I began noticing that this guy who was checking me out and doing his best not to be noticed, was getting closer and closer to me. I realized what he was doing; he was trying to make his move and come over and talk to me. This made me nervous. Finally, he walked up and stood next to me. Picking up an item off the shelf he looked at it for a moment, looked at me and smiled; then he said the scariest most horrific thing I had ever heard anybody say to me, "How are you this evening?" I immediately thought "Ok, I'd seen enough, time to go home," I made my way toward the door and didn't look back. I knew he was intensely watching me as I walked out, and probably undressing me with his eyes. The truth is, my reasoning for hurrying out of there was because I was just scared; this guy was actually trying to make his move and hit on me. Now physically I'm a big guy and could've easily squashed him with my fists, but for some reason, like most guys who aren't gay, I felt very uncomfortable and nervous in this stranger's presence, like I had to get away from this man A.S.A.P. He was a gay man who was going to hit on me, so in my mind, he might as well have been a serial killer with an ax in his hand who was getting too close. I wasn't homophobic by any means. Throughout my life, I've known a lot of gay men who were attracted to me and that never bothered me. In my prime yes I was an attractive man, and I understood that men and women alike were drawn to me because of that. But this was the only time I felt a gay man was going to get too close and try to push up on me, and I had to get away, fast!

From the time I walked outside of the store to unlocking my car door to starting my car and putting it in reverse, I never took my eyes off the front door. I thought he would come out of it and try to make his move in the parking lot. As I began to drive, I relaxed a little more, realizing that I was just trippin' and blowing this situation way out of proportion. It's funny how you can let a thought escalate in your mind and create a life of its own and make you unsettled, but I did. Plus I've suffered from OCD my whole life, so that didn't help. Sometimes I can control it, and sometimes I can't. The point I'm making is people who suffer from OCD know your mind can amplify anything and run with it.

As I continued driving home, I stopped at Mickey D's and pulled into the drive through. While waiting for my turn, I was looking down playing with the radio stations. When I rose my head up, I saw a car driving by me extremely slow. My heart began racing when I saw who was driving the car. It was the man from the adult book store! We were locked in eye-to-eye contact as he slowly drove by me. I knew this was no coincidence that he just happened to pull up next to me at this particular Mickey D's because this city is not that small. It was evident that he had followed me from the adult book store. I watched intently as his car pulled out of the parking lot and into the street. I kept my eyes on his vehicle as he went through the green light and disappeared.

A few days had passed, and I had dismissed the incident as "one of those things" and moved on. So on this day I went to the grocery store to pick up some items, and while standing in the middle of the cereal aisle, I looked to my left and saw a man walking in my direction. It was the gay man again! "What the fuck?" were the words that mumbled from my lips. He didn't even look at me, he came about one quarter through the aisle, looked at an item and turned around and left. "I don't believe it; this mutha fucka is following me," I said to myself. I stood in the aisle for a few minutes longer contemplating my next move and thinking about what was going on here. "Can this man be following me?" I thought to myself, "I think I'm gonna have to confront him, but what if I'm wrong, and it's just a coincidence, and he just happened to be in the same place at the same time as me?"

I decided to walk around the store to see if I could find him. What I would do if I found him I didn't know just yet, but I was looking for him. I went up and down every aisle and even into the bathroom, but he was nowhere to be found. "He must have left the store," I thought. Deciding to give up searching for him, I paid for my groceries and left as well.

About two weeks later, I went on a movie date with one of my friends with benefits. The theater was packed, and we had to sit in one of the back rows. I was sitting about four seats in from the aisle. While enjoying the movie, I saw a person walking up the aisle heading towards the door. As this person got closer, not only could I see that it was a man, but again it was the gay man! Even in the dark, he might as well have had a spotlight on him because I could see him clearly. As he made his way to the door, he looked directly at me, raised his right arm in the air and smiled and waved at me. "This mutha' fucka' is clowning me," I said out loud, "Who is," my friend asked, I didn't answer her, I just replied, "I'll be right back." Mad as hell, I jumped out of my chair and rudely climbed over the people in their seats who were in my way and apologizing at the same time and raced towards the doors. When I got into the theater lobby, all I saw were some people buying food at the snack counter and a woman on the pay phone. I ran into the bathroom, but it was empty. Still infuriated I ran outside to the parking lot, I didn't see him. I walked around the cars to see if I could spot him standing around or possibly sitting in one of the cars. I came up empty. After awhile I realized he got the better of me, and I was going to have to eat this one. I was sure more than ever that this man was fuckin' with me. But why? Just because he finds me attractive? "I'm going to have to be quicker next time and go after him when I see him; don't stall," I thought. I went back inside and finished the movie.

Four days had gone by, and there was no sign of the gay man, but I was starting to become obsessed with him and couldn't get the strange encounters out of my head. I had this strange feeling that I would see him again; he didn't disappoint. I was cleaning out the trunk of my car when a jogger ran by my apartment. I saw him but didn't pay much attention to him. Then about fifteen minutes later, he ran by my apartment again, I saw him a second time and again didn't pay any attention to him. Fifteen minutes later, he ran by my apartment again when my head was buried in the trunk of my car. This time, he spoke to me and asked, "How are you this afternoon?" Instantly I lifted my head up and looked in the direction where the voice was coming from. When I saw the face of the voice, I realized that it was him! He stared back at me with a big easy going smile. Without hesitation I ran after him and yelled, "Come here mutha fucka!" He ignored me and just kept jogging. I was pissed off and ready to handle him. I knew at this point that I was past confrontation; I was going to have to get physical when I caught him. I was so mad that I could already see myself beating his ass and him on the ground. Not because he was gay, but because he was stalking and mocking me. But the oddest thing was happening. He was only jogging and not running fast at all; I was hauling ass, but it was as if I was moving in slow motion and wasn't getting any closer to him. He had to have known that I was coming after him as he continued jogging, but he casually ran as if he didn't have a care in the world? In my past, I've easily out run police and police dogs with no problems, now all of a sudden I can't even catch some white guy who's casually jogging down the street. I had a moment of clarity and realized I couldn't catch this man. I just gave up, and he continued his running stroll as if he never even knew I was chasing him. Completely out of breath I was beyond weirded out by what just happened. I felt that something strange was going on. It was no longer just about some gay guy I ran into at an adult bookstore; something else was happening, but what?

About a month later, I decided to put on my 75-pound weight vest and take a power walk on the bike trail to get some exercise. By then I had let the gay man situation in my mind go. It was what it was I figured. While I was power walking and enjoying the music on my CD player, I felt that there was something creeping up behind me. I turned around and saw the biggest pit bull I had ever seen running directly at me at full speed. It was huge and brown and looked like it ate small kittens like Skittles. Cujo had nothing on this dog when it came to scary and ugliness. He was frightening. I could feel the bass coming off of its growl, and I was scared shitless. As it charged full throttle at me, I looked around to see what my options were. I couldn't run through the woods because I wouldn't be able to out dodge him through the trees, plus if I got too deep in the woods this dog might kill me there and nobody might find me for days. I couldn't climb the trees because the branches were too thin and weak and couldn't hold my weight. At that very moment, I knew I was going to have to fight this dog and kill it by choking its neck. That was if I was lucky enough to get the opportunity to get a hold of its neck. As I braced myself for this attack I felt a body behind me, I quickly turned around and saw that it was, of all people, the gay man! Boy, I was glad to see him this time. For some reason, I wasn't even concerned as to what he was even doing there; after all, he had a habit of popping up at the weirdest times. Still, I had a new option. I could start running and let the dog tear into the gay man's asshole. Sure he outran me before, but he also had a head start. I could leave him in the dust, and he would deserve it for stalking me. However, the man spoke to me, and he said, "Don't be scared. Point to the dog and tell it to stop; it'll listen to you!" At this point, I was willing to entertain anything to get out of this scary situation. I pointed to the dog and yelled at it, "Stop!" and it did. All of a sudden, what was a mean looking dog had softened up and had the cutest innocent look on its face, almost as if to say, "I just want to play?"

The dog continued just to stare at me non-threatening and was now also sitting down as if waiting for a treat. Then the gay man said, "Now tell it to go home." Still pointing at it and scared, I said, "Go home!" The dog calmly stood up, turned around and just walked away. I exhaled like I never had before and could feel all of the energy leave my body from being emotionally drained from the whole scary situation. When I turned around to talk to the man, he was gone. He had just vanished. It was just me surrounded by air, empty space and trees. That's when I realized that the man who I thought was stalking me turned out to be some sort of guardian angel who was watching over and protecting me. I never saw that guardian angel again, but I know he still watches over me.

I thought I had all of the answers and knew everything until I met the man who did. And he sounded more foolish than me.

11

YOU EVER GET THE FEELING YOU'RE BEING WATCHED? WELL DUH

One evening I decided to make my monthly trip to the local adult bookstore to get copies of my two favorite magazines which I was a collector that featured the finest and hottest nude black women of the time.

I jumped into my new Honda Prelude that I had just purchased a week before. It was my first Honda; not only did the engine purr like a kitten, but it was also great on gas. It was snowing fiercely that night, and as I drove to the adult bookstore in the blizzard, I thought about how grateful I was to have a car that handled so well on the ice. I pulled into the parking lot of the store and drove around back so as not to be seen by anyone driving by that might know me, especially from the church. As I entered the store everything was normal, the store lights were dim, and there was a mist of smoke in the air, though I didn't see anybody smoking.

Some of the guys in there were trying to shamefully keep a low profile while other guys were openly shopping like they were at a grocery store. The place reeked and smelled of cleaning products and bleach, probably because of all the men masturbating in the private video booths that needed constant cleaning. Behind the counter was the cliché creepy looking guy who worked the cash register who could pass for a serial rapist? I know in the states they have adult bookstores that are big, open and brightly lit, but at this time in Anchorage, Alaska, most adult bookstores were dark, hole in the wall businesses.

I began making my way to the rack where my beautiful nude black women's magazines waited for me. As I trailed the rack with my eyes, something strange began to happen. I could hear a voice telling me to get out of there. It was so pertinent that I couldn't ignore it, but I couldn't understand why I was hearing a voice telling me to get out. I stood there, not sure as to what to do. Then all of a sudden the room began to spin, it was like a whirlwind, and I was stuck in the middle of it watching everything moving in a fast circle. I saw this with my own eyes. Then it got faster and faster. I felt myself becoming dizzy. At that moment, I felt a force pushing my back towards the direction of the back door that I had entered. I couldn't have gone against the force pushing me even if I wanted to; it was that strong. I didn't fight what was happening to me I just went with it as I was being escorted or should I say forced out the back door by an unseen presence that obviously didn't want me there and meant business. As I went through the back door and ended up on the other side, I heard the door slam shut hard behind me. It was a loud thunderous slam for such a thin, weak door; almost as if it were making a statement.

I was outside. The night was quiet, and I could see my breath was thick in the air, but it wasn't cold. I no longer heard the voice; the spinning had stopped, and the force that was pushing me had released me. "Wow, that was weird?" I thought to myself. Regardless of what just happened, I knew I wasn't going back into that place again that night. "Maybe they had a gas leak, and I hallucinated what just happened," I joked to myself. Either way, it was time to get out of there. I jumped into my car. I put the key in the ignition, and that's when my night began to go downhill because when I turned the key, nothing happened, my car wouldn't start. I repeatedly turned the key back and forth, and still, nothing happened. There was no sound, not even a twitching noise from the ignition, and the dashboard lights didn't come on. The car was completely dead.

I looked under the hood and began twisting and adjusting the battery cables, I got back into the car and tried to start it, and again it was still dead. I started getting pissed. I couldn't believe it. Not only was my new car dead, but it died right outside of an adult bookstore. How embarrassing. "This is fuckin' great!" I yelled among other things. I began swearing and shouting at the top of my lungs and throwing a fit. This was the last thing I needed to happen or the place. I started to calm down and relax a little, then, I felt God speak to me, by way of an impression. He said, "It was Me, and I'm not happy with where you're at." God was letting me know loud and clear that He didn't want me at that adult bookstore. At that moment I knew what I had done wrong and what I needed to do to make it right. I took my hands off the steering wheel and took the key out of the ignition and placed it on the passenger seat. I totally relaxed myself and my mind and began to make peace with what was happening, meaning the lesson I was learning. I took a deep breath and shamefully spoke to God. I said, "Father, I'm sorry for coming here - I made a mistake. I will never come here again. I just want my car to start, and I want to go home." After I had said those heartfelt words to God out loud, I picked up the key off the passenger seat, I put it in the ignition, and when I turned the key, the car started instantly. "Wow God, You work fast," I said out loud as I began to smile. I went home like I told God I would and never returned to that adult bookstore again.

Every star in the sky whether it's dim or shines brightly is accounted for by God. Just like every person on earth, whether their light is dim or shines brightly is accounted for by God.

12

LADY AT THE PARK

One evening around the summer of 1994 while at home, I was bored. I couldn't get a hold of any of my boys. Also, one of my favorite syndicated shows, The Jefferson's, wasn't being shown that night and was replaced by a long, boring infomercial about a new cleaning product for clothes. I had two choices, I could sit on my couch and just channel surf all night, or I could play with myself until I fell asleep. As not to let my evening go to waste, I manifested a third option. I decided to call up my friend Tonya to see if she was interested in a booty call. We spoke for a minute, and she told me to come over to her apartment. I wasted no time getting there. After Tonya and I had done the deed, we had both fallen asleep.

While sleeping, in my mind I could see my spirit quickly moving through the city of Anchorage to a particular destination, but I didn't know where I was going. Even though everything around me was whipping by me at light speed, I could still identify everything that I was passing and seeing. Then, everything began to slow down. I could see myself approaching a local park that was about a half a mile away from my house. I knew the park well. The park was completely empty. There was no sound and even the creek that went along side the bike trail was quiet. I also saw a picnic table that was empty. My mind's eye became focused on this picnic table and stayed there. After awhile, the image began to disappear, and I woke up.

I gently rolled out of bed so as not to wake Tonya, who was snoring like a mountain man, and went to the bathroom. Staring into the mirror, I reflected a little bit of the dream I just had, but still I just brushed it off as one of those things. After using the bathroom, I climbed back into bed and fell asleep. I began to dream, and again my mind wasted no time going back to the same park and also to the same empty picnic table. My mind's eye hovered over the table and knew that there was some sort of pain that was attached to this area, but of what kind of pain I didn't know. And again the image disappeared, and I woke up. As I sat up in bed, I thought to myself that it was odd for me to have the same dream twice in one night, and also for me to remember it. I usually don't remember my dreams when I wake up but usually later that day or week my mind will bring it back to remembrance. However, in this case, that park and that picnic table were stapled to my brain. Still, I didn't read too much into the dream, after all, it was only a park and a picnic table.

At this point, since I was having such a hard time falling asleep, I decided to watch TV. When nothing was on that I cared to watch, being the inconsiderate asshole I was, I decided to try and wake up Tonya for another round of "bumping uglies." I tried turning her on by kissing her neck but she was nonresponsive, so I gave up and focused on going back to sleep. Finally, I fell asleep, and again without missing a beat I was right back at the park and looking at the same picnic table, only this time, something was different. There was a woman sitting at the table. I couldn't see her face, body or even what position she was sitting. I just saw in my mind's eye that there was a woman at the table, and she was in a lot of emotional pain. I felt her pain; I felt the torment that she was going through and that she was in her own personal hell. I wanted to help her but didn't know how to. I wanted to reach out to her with my hand, but I couldn't touch her. All I could do was absorb all of her pain and anguish. Then something terrible began to happen. I felt myself leaving her and my body trying to wake up. "No!" I yelled. I wasn't ready to leave just yet. "I know I can help her just let me try, give me just a little more time, let me stay!" I yelled out to whatever higher being that I knew and felt was there but didn't know who or what it was that I was talking to. "Let me stay with her! I can help her, why won't you let me help her, please let me stay!" I yelled out one last time. Then I woke up.

When I opened my eyes, my mind was still trying to get a grasp on the situation. As I began to fully wake up and realizing that it was just a dream, I was still overwhelmed with sadness for the strange lady. I could still feel her pain and the hurt she carried inside of her as if she were a friend in the room with me. I felt guilty because I wanted to help her but couldn't. Even though she didn't know me and nor I her, and it was just a dream, I felt like I had let her down. I didn't like the way I was feeling, at all. There had to be something I could do to help the poor woman in my dream and to take her pain away. Then, the answer hit me hard, and I felt convicted. I would get out of bed and go to the park and see if she was still there. Yes, I know I was being really silly, and it was only a dream and the idea of going to a park across town at 4:30 in the morning was even sillier but I was convicted and worst case scenario I needed the closure of this dream and about this woman.

I left Tonya's apartment and began driving home; I wanted to stop there first to grab my Bible. I started drilling myself and asking myself questions like, "What are you doing? It was just a dream, and you're getting too caught up in this. When you get home, just jump into bed and pass out. Just forget about it." As I pulled into my drive way and turned the car off, I continued talking to myself, "Maybe I am just trippin' and getting emotionally caught up in the idea of this woman and dream. After all, I have dreams that feel real all the time, but I don't jump up out of bed in the early morning hours to pursue and investigate them. But something is different about this dream. It's almost like God himself is talking to me. I can't shake this feeling or conviction. I don't want to go to this park; I'm dead fuckin' tired, but I feel like I have to go."

I ran into my apartment, changed out of my sex smelling clothes, put on my sweat suit, put my Bible into my backpack, carried my mountain bike outside and rode to the park on the bike trail. All the way there, I kept thinking to myself that I was being stupid and ridiculous, but still, I had an itch that needed to be scratched.

As I pulled up to the park, I could hear the creek that ran next to the bike trail. I could see the early morning birds walking on the grass having their breakfast of bugs. The park was empty and quiet except for a few morning joggers that ran on the trail. Then I looked to my right, and what I saw next made me stop blinking. There, was the picnic table I had seen in my dream, and sitting at it was a lady. At that moment, I knew why I was there. As I approached the table, I stared at the strange woman who was just sitting there oddly all by herself. Her arms were folded and her head buried in them. She had long black hair, and her clothes were dirty.

I didn't say anything to her. I sat down at the table, took out my Bible and pretended to read it just to see what her reaction was going to be, or to see if she was even awake. Ten minutes had gone by, and I began to wonder if I should maybe say something or even nudge her, but before I could do anything she raised her head up. She looked at me, smiled and said, "Hello." Instantly I could smell that she had been drinking. I could also see that she was an Alaskan native in her early forties. I smiled back and said "Hello." Still smiling, she asked, "Are you here for me?" "Yes, I believe I am," I replied. "Are you here to help me?" she asked. I replied, "I'm going to try." Her smile disappeared, and her face began to wither as tears formed in her eyes and started rolling down her cheeks. I kept my composure and asked her what was wrong. She said, "I asked God to help me or send someone that would help me, and He did." When she stated that, I began to feel overwhelmed. It's not that I didn't want to help her, but I wondered "How do I even begin to help this woman?" I didn't even know what her problem was or what she's going through, and I was already feeling overwhelmed. At that moment I had an impression in my mind, God was speaking to me, and He said, "You won't help her, it is not you who does it, but Me." I heard His voice loud and clear. After that, I felt at peace, and I had a better understanding of the situation I was dealing with.

Sympathetically I asked her what was wrong, without hesitance, she said, "The demons, they won't leave me alone." "What are they doing to you," I asked. "They surround me all the time, they attack me every day, I just want peace again, and I want them to leave me alone." Though she reeked of alcohol, I could tell in only her few short words that her mind was alert to her problem. She knew what she was dealing with and what she wanted. And though she appeared emotionally staggered, she still had an inner strength that said, "I'm still here and fighting; I won't go down Satan." Even in her beat up state-of-mind, I felt at that moment that she was still probably spiritually stronger than I was. I was impressed. I asked her, "Do you read your Bible or have a church home?" "No, but my mom reads the Bible a lot," she replied. "Well, I guess it's safe to assume that your mother prays for you all the time, and that's why you made it this far in life," I replied.

At that moment, God had shown me that I was there for the sole purpose of given this woman encouragement because He had plans for her, and also that if I trusted Him, she would receive Him. This woman was hurting and under attack so I decided not to waste any more time. I took a deep breath and let God take the driver's seat. Like an exterminator about to get rid of rodents, I told this woman that we were going to exercise these demons out of her life once and for all. She cried even harder and said, "I'm scared; they want to kill me." Sternly I said, "They can want all they want, but you're God's child, and they won't have their way with what's His. And soon you're going to help others in the same way I'm helping you today. That's why these demons want to kill you, not because of who you are, but who you belong to. And they don't want you to blossom into the spiritual soldier that they know you'll become." I had no idea or knowledge about exercising demons or as to what I was even talking about. All I knew was that God was just using me to speak to and help her, so at the very least I knew how to submit to Him. I grabbed her hands and squeezed them tight. I was dead serious as I prayed loud and hard. I told every demon that was in and around her life that she belonged to the Father of Jesus, and they would not have their way with her.

"You demons recognize God's love for this child sitting here, and that's why you want to destroy her! You see how much the Father adores this child, and that's what makes you detest her so much. You demons see that in the future she will be your worst enemy, and she will expel you out of the lives of others who you will attempt to envelop and destroy. You will not find rest or a place of comfort in her because only God's power can dwell inside of her, not your dark influence that brings uncertainty and a filthy film that stains the inside of a man or woman like dried up syrup on a wall. You can't have her! How dare you try to take what rightfully belongs to God. How dare you try to steal from God. You deceive and lie to each other, but now you think you can bring that evil and deceitfulness inside of what God has created. If a mother bear that has no sense of logic would fight to the death to protect her cubs, do you think the Father who has infinite wisdom and endless love would let anything happen to his daughter? Do you not recognize that this is the Lord's daughter? Of course, you do, that's why you're here. You have no place here, you have no place here, you have no place here!"

I prayed for her for at least a half an hour. As I continued challenging the dark forces, the woman continued to yell and scream louder. Tears streamed down her face as even I could see that the demons that had a hold on her were letting her go. I could actually see dark negative energy leaving her body. God's plan was working. She seemed to be in spiritual pain from this, but I didn't stop. And the louder she screamed, the more I pushed. Then, after awhile she stopped screaming, lowered her head and breathed heavily. She was adjusting to being released. I didn't speak to or rush her. I just let her come down on her own.

When it was all over, our roles were reversed. All of a sudden, she was smiling, and I mean brightly. I was emotionally drained and withered as if I were beaten up by twelve men. I had never done anything like that before. Not so much that I thought it was me, but letting God use me for this spiritual battle. I was emotionally drained. Looking at the woman, I couldn't believe how radiant she was, and all it took was for someone to pray for her to be released. The alcohol that had a hold of her mental state was now gone; now she was speaking clearly. Her eyes looked right through me, and the dark energy that radiated off of her body was now a bright aura.

I wrote down some scriptures and page numbers for her to read and handed her my Bible. I told her that soon she would be helping others the way that she was helped here today. And it was important for her to start reading her new Bible and learn how the Father wants to work in her life. I stood up but could barely stay upright or keep my balance from exhaustion, but we embraced in one last hug and a moment of gratitude from both of us and to the Father. She kissed me on the cheek, and we departed.

*Love, understanding, patience and forgiveness. Why do
I always ask for what I won't give in return?*

13

JIMMY

James Felix aka Jimmy was my best friend. In fact, we were more like brothers. We met at the age of twelve in the 7th grade at Romig junior high school in Anchorage, Alaska. One day in between classes Jimmy approached me and said, "Hey, you wanna ride bikes after school?" "Yea, sounds cool," I said. So on that day in early October 1986 would begin a bond between two twelve-year-olds that would last for sixteen years. Instantly we were drawn to each other. I liked him the first time I met him. I thought he was a loud mouth, full of energy and the funniest kid I had ever met. He liked me because I was cocky, good looking and had a way with the girls. I guess he thought while hanging out with me he would meet girls, after all, I was a pretty boy and he wasn't. I had the looks and also the arrogant personality.

We had a divine connection and shared everything. If one of us had more money than the other, we would put the money together and divide it so we would be equal. We also had an unconditional loyalty to each other almost like brothers; I had his back, and he had mine. Our friendship was fast and automatic. Some people have soul mates, well we were soul friends.

Jimmy had this uncanny ability to be spontaneously funny at any moment. He was so funny that it was almost weird and freaky to me at times that anybody could be that funny for no reason. He had the humorous tongue and animation that I compare to Richard Pryor, and Chris Tucker wrapped into one. To this day I have never met anybody who is as funny, animated, and outgoing as Jimmy was. His humor was divine, spiritual and a gift from God. People loved to be around him and be in his presence just to see what he was going to say or do next. I've seen Jimmy walk into the presence of hardcore Compton gang bangin' killers with mean mugging bad attitudes and within minutes Jimmy had them all coming out of their shells and falling over laughing. He just had that gift and charisma to make anybody laugh. I still think of something he said or did over twenty years ago and laugh my ass off like it was brand new.

Most people that know me know that I've been a fan of the rock group Kiss for most of my life. I'll never forget the look on Jimmy's face the first time I brought him over to my house. It was two months into our friendship when he walked into my room and was bug-eyed when he saw that my bedroom walls and ceiling were covered in Kiss posters. It was the funniest thing to see his expression because he had never heard of a black person who liked Kiss. He just looked at my room with shock and amazement. Then he spoke, "You like Kiss?" "Yea, since I was five, I collect everything with Kiss' name on it," I said. Then he put his hand on my shoulder and gave me a look of sorrow, and jokingly, he said, "You know what, it doesn't matter, you still my nigga, but don't worry, we're gonna get you some help? There's a ten step program for weird niggas like you." I laughed so hard after that funny comment, that I knew we were going to be best friends forever.

We were inseparable and did everything together. We hung out at the malls, movies, arcades. We had this trick that we used to do at the teen night club. The admission was five dollars to get in, and we would split the cost. Since Jimmy was darker than me, he would go in first and pay for the admission and get the back of his hand stamped. Then before the ink would dry he would quickly come out the back door where I would be waiting, and we'd press the back of our hands together so I would have the stamped image and enter the club. We thought we were geniuses, and also thought we were the first people in the history of the world to come up with this idea.

At this time in America, mid 80's, rap music was becoming more mainstream and popular on MTV. Thanks to groups like Run DMC and the Beastie Boys. We loved all of it. Jimmy and I started our own act, which was lip singing to Run DMC songs. He always did Run's lyrics, and I was always DMC. Every once and awhile one of our friends would fill in as DJ Jam Master J for us if we were lucky. We would participate in all the talent shows at the malls, school, and recreation centers. Because our older brothers had the latest and better gear than we had we would steal their Kangol hats, bomber jackets and Adidas shoes to perform in. Sure the clothes were always bigger on us, and it looked like we were melting in them, sure we would have to take a few punches from our older brothers for stealing their clothes but we loved entertaining, and it was worth it to hear those girls screaming for us when we were on stage. Jimmy and I were together, taking on the world and doing our thing. But what we loved to do more than anything in the world was stealing cars. Nothing and I mean nothing made us happier. It's a major rush when you're a young man behind the wheel of a vehicle doing sixty down the highway.

One day during lunch hour at school, Jimmy approached me and told me as soon as school gets out at 2:45 to go straight to the Burger King two blocks away and wait for him because he wants to show me something. I made it to the Burger King at 3:00 and Jimmy arrived driving a Subaru station wagon and blasting the radio. He pulled up next to me, laughing and smiling, "Come on, get in." While in his social studies class, when the teacher wasn't paying attention, Jimmy took her keys and money out of her purse. So now we were driving in a stolen car that belonged to one of our teachers and spending her money. As a young man, I got my first taste of being in a stolen car and it was fun, exciting and an adrenaline rush. At the end of the day, we parked his teacher's car two blocks away from the school and wrote "FUCK YOU BITCH" on the windshield with lipstick that we found in the glove compartment. Jimmy didn't like this particular teacher because she kept giving him detention.

That incident would only be the beginning of many episodes for our new found love of stealing cars. We had just gotten our first taste of being car thieves and getting away with it. Like a wolf that tasted blood for the first time, we wanted more. For us stealing cars and just being a thief period represented freedom. We got what we wanted without paying for it. Plus, we were both poor so we got to stick it to those who had more than we did and we enjoyed it. Jimmy and I also had a rule, if we could help it, we wouldn't steal from anybody black, old, or under-privileged. For instance, one day we stole a Cadillac then later realized it belonged to an elderly white couple, we felt really bad after we realized who we had stolen it from. So we took the Cadillac to the car wash and washed and detailed the inside and outside really good. We also checked all the fluids under the hood and filled up the gas tank. Later that night we parked the car in front of their house and got out and ran.

Sometimes there were funny incidents that would happen like the time we were driving in a dangerous snowstorm in a stolen truck. I lost control of the vehicle, and the truck got stuck in a snow bank. We spent twenty minutes trying to get it out, but it wouldn't budge. A patrol car with two officers inside pulled up beside us. They had a police dog in the back so trying to run was pointless especially in the snow. One of the officers asked, "You boys stuck?" I responded, "Yeah, it's really slick out here." "Well here. We'll give you a hand." These two cops were actually helping us get our stolen truck out of the snow bank! It was pretty funny. They never asked our age or for any I.D. We thanked them and drove off.

Another time Jimmy and one of our deceased partners Fred, (RIP) and I were looking in a movie theater parking lot for a car to steal. We were spread out so none of us knew what the other was doing. Fred screeches around the corner in a Monte Carlo, and we jumped in and took off. Now normally to break down the key ignition, you would use a screwdriver or a butter knife. We drove for about three blocks when we asked Fred how he got the car because none of us had a screwdriver or a butter knife. He responded, "Oh, I used this Jesus cross that was hanging from the rearview mirror." Jimmy and I looked at each other like we had just seen Jesus himself. Jimmy asked, "You mean you used a Jesus cross to break down the ignition?" Fred said, "Yeah. So what? Stop acting like scared bitches. Ain't nothing gonna happen." As soon as he completed that sentence, he grabbed his neck and began making gagging noises. The car was doing about 45 mph, and Fred let go of the wheel. I grabbed it trying to keep the car steady and telling him to hit the brake. Fred was apparently choking on the big wad of gum he had been chewing on all night. I tried to reach my foot over to step on the brake, but Fred's leg was in the way. I looked at his face, and his eyes were completely red. Either his gum was going to kill him or this car was going to kill us all. Finally, the wad of gum shot out of his mouth and landed on the dashboard. At that young age, I wasn't religious at all, but even I knew you don't use a Jesus cross to still a car, but Fred had to learn the hard way.

I was still holding on to the wheel while Fred struggled to catch his breath. Then we saw police lights behind us. They obviously saw the car swerving on the road. Fred pulled the car into the middle of the highway and gunned it. The police were right behind us and not letting up. Then, two more cops joined the pursuit. The car began overheating, and we knew it wouldn't hold out much longer, so he pulled into a neighborhood, we jumped out of the car and scattered.

After jumping over eight fences, I found a dog house where I could hide. The police were all over the neighborhood, and they multiplied to what now seemed like a hundred. For all they knew, we had just robbed a liquor store. I sat in that dog house for a least two hours freezing and wondering if I should try to run or even give myself up because I was losing the battle with Jack Frost. Finally, I came up with an idea. It was risky but worth a shot. I took my clothes off and only wore my t-shirt, boxer shorts, shoes, and socks. I grabbed the dog leash and walked directly in the street where all the cops were, yelling out, "Bandit, come here! Bandit, where are you?" A cop approached me and asked me what I was doing. I said, "I'm just looking for my dog." He asked me if I had seen three guys running through the neighborhood. I told him I hadn't seen anyone, and I had just come out of my house when I noticed my dog wasn't in the yard. He let me go. I walked home just like that, wearing next to nothing. None of us got caught.

Another funny moment was when Jimmy, myself and some associates of ours went to a car dealership at night. The plan was simple and very stupid, break out the side window which was tall and wide, run in, jump in a car and drive out, no mathematics required.

Well, Thompson was the biggest guy in the group and the oldest. He picked up a big boulder rock over his head and threw it at the window. What we didn't know was the window was a very thick piece of glass that bullets probably wouldn't have penetrated. So, like something out of a cartoon, the big boulder rock bounced off the window and hit Thompson in the head knocking him unconscious. There was a pool of blood pouring out of his head but still everybody was on the ground laughing their asses off, especially Jimmy. It was the funniest thing any of us had ever seen. We had to take him to the emergency room and in time he healed. We didn't get to steal any cars that night but the laughter compensated for it. Thompson, if you're reading this, I'm sorry, but it was funny.

Jimmy and I decided it was time to up our street credentials and do something bigger and bolder, rob a bank! Now, remember we're teenagers. The plan was Jimmy would go into the bank with a letter demanding cash, and I would drive the getaway car. So when the big day came, I waited in the parking lot of the bank. Jimmy had already been inside for a few minutes, and then a few minutes turned into an hour. At this point I was way past nervous because I didn't know if he had gotten caught or if security was holding him down and waiting for the police, a million thoughts raced through my head. But one thing I couldn't do was leave him. If I saw him being escorted out in handcuffs that would be a different story, but until then I had to chill. Finally, after what seemed like an eternity, he calmly walked out of the bank empty handed. I asked, "What happened? What took you so long?" He replied, "Well, when I got to the counter I got really nervous and had to shit really bad, so I asked the lady where the bathroom was. By the time I finished, I had lost my nerve." We looked at each other for a few seconds and then busted out laughing. I think when it came to the idea of bank robbery we were in way over our heads. We never tried that again.

It wasn't always about us being mischievous. What we also loved doing was taken a stolen car that we were driving in, stop at a fast food joint, order a bunch of food, drive to the richer neighborhoods and just park and stare at the beautiful houses. Jimmy and I had this obsession with beautiful houses. We were probably the only two teenagers in the world who would actually buy magazines that featured mansions and big luxury homes. We would just sit in our stolen car in what we called "the white neighborhoods" eating our food and talking about our fantasies about living in one of these big homes one day when we became rich and famous. Jimmy would always say things like he was going to buy a whole block so all of his family members could live in one place and be together. He would also jokingly say that he wanted to have mountain bikes to hang upside down from the ceiling of his garage, just like the rich white people have in their garages. He said he would never ride them; they would be there just for show. I would crack up when he would make comments like that. We weren't bad kids by any means. We were just two kids who needed an escape from the dysfunction at home.

My car stealing days would finally catch up with me and come to an end. What would be my last car theft came about by a bunch of us jumping a gated fence into a car lot/dealership. I was inside a Nissan trying to break down the ignition with my screwdriver; then I heard Jimmy yell, "Run!" I looked up, and there were cops everywhere! My friend Tyson and I ran to the fence and jumped up at the same time hitting our heads together like coconuts. After hitting the ground, we got up again and jumped over the fence and ran like hell! I ran for 2 miles, and I was only a block away from my apartment building. I saw a lot of police cars racing around. They obviously saw me running in that direction.

I decided to lay down flat on a slanted hill and wait until the smoke had cleared. I was already thinking about what I was going to eat and what shows were on TV. All of a sudden, I was attacked by a police dog! The dog bit me all over my back and arms, and the cops who showed up just stood there watching him do it. I fought the dog off as hard as I could, but his teeth were ripping into my hands and arms until my blood was all over his face. Finally, they pulled the dog off of me, handcuffed me and took me to a police substation. When the lead officer asked them how I got the blood all over me, the arresting officer said, "We found him like this. He must have fell or something." Because he was the fastest runner in the group Jimmy got away. I was locked up for a week, and I hated every second of it. I told myself I would never get locked up again especially over car theft. So just like that, I quit stealing cars.

As the years went on and we got older, the bond between Jimmy and I became even tighter. He came to accept my Kiss obsession, and when he would travel out of state, he would always bring me back a Kiss t-shirt or a Kiss item. Even in our early/mid-twenties we would still talk and joke on the phone like a couple of teenage girls or sit on the phone with each other watching a TV show or movie. Or when one of us would drop the other off at his house we would sit in the car for hours just talking about our dreams and plans of making it big in the entertainment business as rappers. The truth is, in our sixteen-year friendship, Jimmy and I had absolutely nothing in common. We didn't like the same things; our interests were way off. I liked dark-skinned black women, and he liked light skinned black women. He preferred noise, and I wanted quiet. But we had this unspoken bond between us to me that was almost spiritual. It was like we were brothers from another mother.

Once in a dream, I saw Jimmy and myself in a past life, Jimmy and I were both white male soldiers in a war. Jimmy had been shot, and I carried him to an abandoned building to nurse him. He was wounded badly, and I felt helpless because I didn't know if I could stop the bleeding. I did everything I could to save him until I realized that all I could do was hold him to comfort him. He died right there in my arms. It was the first time I would know what it feels like to let down a loved one, even if it was in a past life. I don't want to get into your religious beliefs or perspectives about past lives, but I didn't feel that it was a dream but a past life remembrance. I saw it as it happened then, not as a dream. Jimmy died in my arms in that war, and in this life, we were given another chance to be friends and to take care of each other.

Jimmy and I both knew what it meant not to have any food in the house and to be on welfare. We were children of the free breakfast and lunch programs at the school. After Jimmy's parents separated for personal reasons his mother had to struggle to take care of all the children and keep food on the table. It wasn't easy for her, and it especially wasn't easy for Jimmy to watch his mother going through such a hard time. As he got older, I believe that's what made Jimmy such a caring and giving person when it came to the homeless or just anybody in need. When homeless people on the streets would ask for spare change, Jimmy would always tell them, "I won't give you any money, but I'll be happy to take you to a store or restaurant, and you can buy or order all the food you want." He would also say "I'll never let a mutha fucka go hungry, I don't care who it is, I know what it's like to go without food!" And he meant it because he's been there.

I also remember a time when Jimmy and I were sitting in his car in the parking lot of my apartment complex. A drunken woman came staggering out of the building and could barely walk. We noticed she had two kids in the car. Jimmy jumps out of the car and approaches the lady and begins talking to her. He comes back to the car and says, "This woman is drunk out of her mind. No way am I gonna let her drive in her condition especially with her kids in the car." So he drove the drunken lady and her children home, and I followed them in his car. When he got them home safely, he put the keys in her mailbox and we left. That was just the kind of good-hearted person he was.

Even though Jimmy and I talked about and shared everything with each other, the one thing he didn't talk with me about was his mother's medical condition. His mother was having serious health issues, and it ate Jimmy up inside. I believe he felt that her time was limited, and it made him feel helpless. He loved his mother more than anything in the world and knew of the sacrifices she had made for him. He just wanted her to be happy in life like most men do when they reach a certain age. Deep down Jimmy wanted to make it big so he could give his mother the life he always felt she deserved. Like all men that want to buy their mother that big house up on the hills, he wanted his mother to live like a queen. Because it was a sensitive subject, I never asked too many questions when it came to his mother's situation, but I was supportive.

One morning in October 2002, Jimmy called me and asked me if I wanted to go to a party up in the Hillside area near the mountains. I told him I couldn't and that I had to work that night. We began talking about our rap group that we were in together, possible upcoming shows and recording new material. I didn't know why but Jimmy sounded different. He had a tone in his voice that was carefree and peaceful. It was strange to me because of all the years I've known him I've never heard him sound the way he did. It was like he had a spiritual calmness about him. Before we hung up with each other, he said something even stranger, "Don't worry about anything, everything is going to be alright." He repeated it one more time, "Everything is going to be alright." It was like he knew something without realizing that he knew it. We said goodbye.

I got off work the following morning around 2:00 a.m. I went home, jumped into bed and quickly fell asleep. Around 6:30 a.m. my phone rang. I was really incoherent when I answered it, but I quickly realized that it was Jimmy's fiancé on the other end. I lived in a security building, and she was downstairs and telling me to come down. I don't know why I did this because I didn't think that anything was wrong, but I hauled ass down those stairs, didn't even try to take the elevator, but something inside of me told me to hurry. When I got to the glass doors, I saw three people, Jimmy's fiancé and two of his sisters. I remember thinking to myself that it was strange for them to be at my apartment at this hour but still I didn't think anything was wrong. When I opened the door, I realized that all three of them had a look of being emotionally lost and sadness on their faces. Jimmy's sister spoke up and said, "Jimmy's not with us anymore."

The three of them were trying to tell me that Jimmy had died in a car accident the night before. Of course, they were all dead wrong. As we spoke in the lobby of my apartment building for about twenty minutes, it still wasn't registering in my mind what they were telling me. Of course, they have to be wrong, and this has to be some sort of mistake. You see, people like Jimmy don't die. He's full of life, personality, makes people smile, plus he's been my best friend and brother for sixteen years. God wouldn't take my brother away from me. I'm not perfect, but I knew God loved me more than that. I remember feeling like I just wanted to go back upstairs and go back to bed, and we can deal with this misunderstanding when the sun comes up. I gave each girl a hug, and they left.

I calmly walked up the stairs and didn't even think about what they had said to me. I grabbed the door handle to my apartment and turned it. I slowly opened up the door and walked inside and closed it. I took a few steps into my living room and that's when it hit me. What they said had finally registered in my brain. Jimmy was dead! I let out a loud yell. I had become hysterical; I began shaking all over. I was hollering and screaming like I never had before, crying uncontrollably. Repeatedly, I yelled out, "Why-why-why-why?"

It hit me as to what to do next. I would ask my Brother Mark if this was true. Mark wouldn't lie to me, especially about this. Again I was hysterical as I ran to the bedroom and grabbed the phone. My shaking hands were trying to dial the long distance number to Flagstaff, Arizona. When I heard my brother's voice answer I urgently said, still crying and shaken, "Mark, they're trying to tell me that Jimmy's dead." He replied, "I already know, it's true." Our Sister Lorraine had already called him to tell him the bad news. The phone fell out of my hand as I let out another yell. Mark had confirmed that my nightmare was really happening. I wanted to yell out, "You're all lying to me!" But Mark wouldn't lie to me. Jimmy had died.

Even to this day, I try not to ask too many details about his death from his family. I guess I don't want to deal with having to hear anything new or be reminded about Jimmy's demise. But the story that was told to me and from the local news was that Jimmy had left a party in the Hillside area. He was driving his new BMW, and he always loved to brag about how fast that car could go. As he rounded a corner, he lost control of the vehicle and spun out of control. When the car finally stopped, a Mustang was approaching fast from behind him, and the driver didn't have enough time to stop. The Mustang had hit his BMW from behind, and Jimmy hit his head on the steering wheel causing his fatality.

The day of the funeral arrived. And still, in my mind I believed that this had to be a mistake and that this couldn't really be happening. This was just one big misunderstanding that could still be cleared up. My older Sister Lorraine drove me to the church where the service was being held. I hated every second of that day. She held my hand as we entered the front door. Since I knew it was going to be an open casket funeral, I stopped and asked her to find out exactly where the coffin was at because I didn't want to accidently see Jimmy's lifeless body and I didn't want that image of him to catch me off guard. She went inside to look and came back and told me where the coffin was located. She grabbed my hand and told me that it was time for me to see him and to say goodbye before they closed the coffin. That was the longest walk of my life. A walk I never thought I would have to take. As I rounded the corner I could see Jimmy lying there in the distance. The closer I got the more my body began to shake and tremble. I stopped only a few feet from him and started to cry. I couldn't believe that I had to see him like this. It was too much for me as I wept uncontrollably. It was Jimmy, but it wasn't Jimmy? My beautiful brother was just lying there in a coffin. Why God, why?

As the service continued, I got a hold of myself and did my best to help out by meeting and greeting people and thanking them for coming. I tried to make sure the people were comfortable and brought water and tissues to those who needed it. The church was full because Jimmy had touched so many different people's lives, and it was great to see such a large turnout for him. Still, I felt a little selfish and bitter on the inside. I remember thinking, "Why are you people even here. You didn't know him the way I did. Half of you I have never even seen before. What gives you the right to be here? He was my best friend, not yours." I was just hurting on the inside and in my mind I needed someone or something to lash out at. The moment came when I would go up to say some words about Jimmy as his best friend. I already knew in my mind what I would say, but when I got behind that microphone, the words just wouldn't come out right. For me, talking about Jimmy in the past tense at his funeral would mean that I would have to admit publicly that this was really happening, and Jimmy had really passed away. I wasn't ready to do that. I just mumbled and tripped over my own words on the mic. Then, I just gave up and ended my speech. To this day, I don't even remember what I said. I just knew that I wanted to get away from that place and away from all the people who kept lying to me and trying to make me believe that Jimmy had really died. I had left the service early and didn't even go to his burial. I don't remember if I was supposed to be a pallbearer or not. I just wanted out.

After Jimmy's death, my entire life changed. Something inside of me broke. His passing was too much for me, and the only way I could deal with it was to suppress it deep inside of me and forget about his death and him. I didn't want to see photos of him, and I wouldn't listen to music tracks that we recorded together with his voice on them. I was doing pretty good until one day I went to his fiancé's house to use her computer and when I walked into the living room, I saw pictures of Jimmy on the walls. Instantly I began to cry and felt ill. I got a hold of myself before she could tell anything was wrong with me. Just looking at pictures of my best friend who was no longer here was just too much for me.

The worst thing you could do when someone you love dies is to suppress your feelings and emotions. Because with suppressed feelings comes major side effects. Besides growing up with OCD, I had never dealt with mental and emotional issues before in my life. All of a sudden I began having panic/anxiety attacks, spontaneously crying and depression. Also, my confidence and self-esteem were dramatically lowered. The days after the funeral, I remember never wanting to go outside. I was actually afraid of being out in the open. I didn't know why. When I would get off work, instead of trying to hurry up and get out of there which was my normal routine, I would make up excuses to hang out at work longer. I would do extra work, help other employees with their duties, or just hang out and talk with co-workers about the stupidest things. I would do anything not to be outside. I think it was because emotionally I didn't trust the world anymore. My reality had been tainted. But above all, I didn't trust God anymore, because He had taken away something that was precious to me.

I was lost and confused and couldn't understand why my friend couldn't be here anymore. I was a take charge individual, I had a lot of initiative and wasn't scared to take chances or get my nails dirty if I had to. I had an insight and intelligence unlike most of my peers, and for fun, I would study psychology and western philosophy. But when it came to death, I was totally immature, lost and perplexed.

At this point in my life, God had become my enemy. I felt that the one being in the world that I always knew that I could count on had totally betrayed me. Sure I wasn't perfect and was anything but righteous and holy and yes I knew I could have made more of an effort to have a stronger relationship with Him. But I always felt regardless God would always have my back and keep His other eye on me including my loved ones. How could He have let such a thing come to pass? He knew Jimmy was my best friend; He knew how close we were, and He should have also known how his death would affect me. Still, He allowed Jimmy's death to happen.

I cursed God every chance I got. He was a liar, a manipulator, someone who said one thing but did something else. Never had I felt this much hatred towards anybody, in the flesh or spirit. I would have moments of fits and anger and would do things that I believed would hurt or offend God. I had pictures of Jesus in my apartment that I kept for protection. I believed as long as I had those pictures of Jesus nothing bad would happen to me. Even when I brought girlfriends over for sex, I would turn those pictures face down or take them off the wall until we were done out of respect. I took all of my pictures of Jesus and ripped them up. I put the torn pieces in the toilet and pissed all over them. "Fuck you God - you piece of shit," I would say as I was urinating. I ripped up my Bible page-by-page, and afterwards I threw them all in the trash, I repeatedly spit on the shredded pages. Sometimes while driving at night if I saw a church I would pull into the parking lot, get out and spit on the building. It might sound a little strange, but I was looking for any excuse to tell God "Fuck you!" I was so full of anger and confusion over Jimmy's death that it ate away at my stomach to the point where I would be in pain. I no longer cared about myself anymore. I was sleeping with girlfriends and female friends and most of the time I wasn't even using condoms. What was the point? You try to be a decent human being, help others when you can, work hard and sacrifice and in the end all you get is death at a young age. "Yea, that's fair God?" So many times while driving fast I would see a brick wall and actually visualize driving into it head on. It wasn't that I was suicidal or wanted to die, I was just so tired of the emotional pain and depression that I just wanted it all to go away.

After awhile I began feeling anger towards Jimmy. I was mad at him for leaving and after everything we had been through together he never even said goodbye. He never said, "See you on the other side" or "Thanks for being my friend in this life." Instead, I just woke up one morning, and he was gone. While growing up together, the plan was never for one of us to die at a young age, but that we would grow up, always take care of each other and take over the world together. I felt like Jimmy had broken that unspoken pact we had between us. Again, he never even said goodbye.

Later, my anger would turn into guilt. I began to feel guilty that Jimmy had died. I would think to myself, "Maybe if I had done something different he would still be here today. What if I would have told him that night not to go to that party, he might still be alive." Yes, we were supposed to look after each other like brothers, and I failed him because he's dead and he's not coming back. I didn't even have the guts to go to his grave to visit and talk to him. As I write this book, I have only been to his grave site one time, and that was about four years after his passing. While I was there, my mind couldn't register the fact that the grave site I was standing over was Jimmy's, so I left.

I even began having the same recurring dreams where I would see Jimmy in public somewhere and when I would yell out his name and run towards him he would quickly walk away from me. Or when I would finally catch up with him he would smile and say that he was busy, but he would meet up with me later. In my dreams, he was always avoiding me. I suppose my guilt was causing these recurring dreams.

I was in such a bad place over Jimmy's death that I ended up on prescription antidepressant medication. Instead of helping me, the medication made me feel worse. My mind had become a roller coaster. One minute I would feel a little better and the next minute I would feel like my whole world was coming to an end. I would call my father, mother, brothers and sisters in the middle of the night and make them all tell me that they loved me. They would calm me down enough so I could at least sleep. Months later, I got a job working out in the oil fields of Alaska, and my boss had to have me fly back home twice due to the depression pills that were having a terrible effect on me and making me more screwed up and depressed than I already was. One night it was so bad that I finally had to check myself into the hospital. My friend Dawn, who's a certified nurse, had to meet me at the hospital to sit with me and talk to the doctors on my behalf. It was embarrassing but necessary. I lived my entire life drug and alcohol-free because the thought of not being in control of my own mind scared me. Now here I was on drugs prescribed by professional doctors, and I ended up turning into a chemically unbalanced nut-job. When all that shit finally flushed out of my system, I swore I would never take antidepressant drugs again no matter how bad I felt. And I never did. Still, my depression continued. There were times where I would be so depressed and low that I felt like I didn't want to be alone. Some nights I would stay the night with friends, or with a girlfriend, or my mom's or sister's house. On one particular night at my sister's house, everything changed.

I retired to the bedroom in my Sister's home. There was no bed in the room, so I made a bed on the floor. I laid there, sideways on my right side in the dark trying to fall asleep. Thoughts of Jimmy began to fill my mind. As usual, I found myself starting to become overwhelmed with sadness. My eyes watered, and the tears began to roll down my face onto the pillow. As I continued to think of Jimmy I became consumed with hurt and guilt. I laid on the floor and sobbed over my friend.

Then something happened. Still lying on my right side and facing the wall, I felt two hands grab my left arm and softly squeeze. I was the only one in the room and if someone would have walked in I would have easily known it. I quickly jerked around, and I saw a greenish light, the light was the size and figure of a man. Instantly I knew it was Jimmy. I jumped up and turned on the light. I yelled out, "Jimmy!" But the room was empty. My heart was racing, I was shaking. I yelled out again, "Jimmy!" I waited for any kind of response from him, a voice, a sign, or an object to move or fall over, but nothing happened. I knew it was Jimmy! How I knew it was Jimmy was I knew what his hands felt like. We grew up play fighting, wrestling, slapping hands and falling over each other laughing. I knew Jimmy's hands. I said his name one last time, a little quieter "Jimmy?" Again, there was no answer. I sat down. Then something even more amazing happened, the room began to fill with the smell of Jimmy's cologne that he always wore. It was as if this was his way of telling me, "Yes Anthony, it's me, and I know that you've been hurting about my death, but I'm ok." The smell of that cologne validated to me what I already knew; Jimmy had visited me in that room that night. I was happy that he came to visit me, and also to know that he was alright. But I was a little disappointed that he didn't stay a little longer and actually make himself more visible to me. I guess I'm just being a little greedy and selfish and should've been happy with the visitation I got from him. I just wanted more because, I missed my best friend.

In God we trust. Except when it comes to my personal life and well-being.

14

GOD, THE REPAIR MAN

I can remember a time when I was extremely mad at God, which in those days seemed like all the time. It was during the winter of 2005. I had become discouraged because I had felt that God wasn't answering my prayers or moving fast enough and at that time I felt I desperately needed help and wasn't receiving it. I was a cook in the oil fields of Prudhoe Bay, Alaska, and my camp had closed down for six months, and I wasn't successful at getting a transfer to another camp or work in town in the city of Anchorage.

I started to feel like God was ignoring me or punishing me for something that I didn't know I did. He knew I was out of work. He knew that money was tight, and I had bills. Also to be trivial He also knew that the radio in my car was broken, and I didn't have the money to buy a new one because I was saving all the money I had for gas. There's nothing I hated more than to drive around with no music or sound in my car. I was feeling the pressure of being out of work. Also, having to borrow money from family and friends was adding to my stress and a little embarrassing. To top it all off, it had only been a few years since my best friend Jimmy had passed away, so I was still in a very sensitive state of mind. Yes, I believed that God had heard my prayers, and He knew what I was going through, but my way of thinking was, "What good did any of that do me if He wasn't helping or answering me?" Especially if the help I wanted wasn't happening in my time frame. Also, I would talk to God out loud and say, "What the hell did I do that was so bad that You would leave me hangin' like this?" At that time I had very little patience and didn't quite know the concept of waiting on God, and "He's not always there when you call, but He's always on time." I felt frustrated and forsaken.

During the last couple of months of my unemployment, I had stopped praying and talking to God, at least in a humble spiritual manner. I was taking a stand. I was protesting I suppose. I didn't see much light at the end of the tunnel. I felt God had failed me, and I wasn't trying to receive anything from Him unless it came in the form of a check with my name on it. I asked Him, "Why should I invest my time and prayers into You if You don't even see fit to help me when I need it."

The only time I would speak to God is when I was complaining or criticizing His work and what He wasn't doing for me. I would cuss Him out, throw fits, and speak to Him as if we were on equal terms. I knew He had heard every word I said especially the swearing and F-bombs I was dropping towards Him. I would say things like, "What the fuck do You do all day 'Mr. a Sparrow won't fall out of the sky' without You knowing about it. You got the time to count dead birds all day, but You can't even take a few minutes to help my black ass? What the fuck are You good for anyway? Killing my best friend in a car accident wasn't good enough for You? What, You're not happy unless You're dragging me through the dirt and watching me suffer?" I would get so mad at Him that sometimes when I would drive I would throw all of my Jesus items out of the car window. It was just a period for me where it was easier to be a brat then it was to go through the long suffering with grace and faith.

One afternoon while shopping at a grocery store, I ran into a friend, Travis, who I haven't seen in at least four years. We went to junior high school together. After giving fist pounds and a hug, we struck up a conversation about our current lives and what we had been up to since we had last seen each other. It was cool to see Travis and catch up on things. Some friends you outgrow as you get older, interest change and you find that you have less and less in common as you mature and evolve. Even though Travis and I weren't the kind of friends that hung out together, he was still the kind of friend who I would always be there for if he needed anything. Travis was always a genuine person, kind-hearted and never meant any harm to anyone. I would always say that if I ever went to jail for five to ten years and gave Travis a million dollars of my money to hold on to for me, I would feel confident in knowing that he would still have every penny waiting for me when I got out. He was just that kind of guy.

As we continued talking, Travis switched the conversation to some problems he was having in his life. I stood there and listened to this humble person telling me about the issues that were bringing him down and making him feel withered. One story was worse than the next. That's when I began to realize that he had a tired, emotional look on his face, a look that said, "My problems are beginning to break me, I'm so tired, but I'm doing the best I can, I'm hanging in there." I began to feel really bad for Travis; he didn't deserve this. Some people reap what they sow, but this guy has such a golden heart that it was just sad, and I was overwhelmed with such a helpless feeling. As I listened to his problems I wanted to help my friend in any way I could but I could barely do anything to help myself at this point. I had my own struggles and issues. I could barely afford the groceries I was buying at the store that day. Besides emotional support, what else could I offer my friend? We exchanged our new phone numbers, and I told him that I would call him soon.

About a week had passed, and I was still frustrated. Of course, my financial situation hadn't gotten any better, and I was still pissed off at God for continuing to be what I called absent. On one particular afternoon, I decided to take a nap for a couple of hours because I had to be at rehearsals with my rap group later that evening. While napping, I had a dream and in this dream, God was talking to me. He was telling me to go to the Christian bookstore and I was to buy particular items for Travis. He also told me He would show me what I was to buy when I got there. He told this to me in my dream through impression. It was so blunt that when I woke up, I had the alert feeling of a man in the service that was just given his orders for my new important, top secret assignment. I became excited because now I knew what I had to do to help Travis. Not only that, but God Himself has designed this mission for me and gave me my orders through a dream. I was ready to do this; I could help my friend.

After a few minutes had gone by, my mind began to bring itself back to my reality. I began to speak to God with an attitude, "Wait a minute, I'm still broke, still out of a job, I'm still struggling and still not getting any help. I'm not going to stand here and get excited or go racing across town to the Christian bookstore and pay for some items that I can't even afford over some stupid dream. I'm struggling right now, and this is how

You choose to intervene in my life? Are You serious or what?" I ignored God's orders and stayed home.

Because I chose to ignore God's demand, over the next week and a half everything began to go downhill for me. My car started giving me problems. Mechanical problems or a bill was the last thing I needed. My TV's cable continued to go out on me due to technical difficulties so I would miss most or all of the NBA games that were on, and I loved watching the games. My refrigerator died, and most of the food inside had to be thrown out. And to top it all off my small unemployment check that was always on time all of a sudden was lost in the mail. Aside from being unemployed, broke, and frustrated, everything else was falling apart. It was like my hedge of protection had been removed from around me, and I was an open target for the demons that had always hovered around my life.

I knew what was going on. God had sent me on an assignment, and I refused to do it. I was deliberately disobeying an order. So to get my attention, He allowed some unpleasant things to take place in my life. I knew things were just going to get worse for me if I continued to refuse God's orders. Sure, before these negative things began to happen I was already an unhappy person, but that level of unhappiness I could handle. But now my unpleasant circumstances were getting more intense. Sometimes I would think that I would have it bad and then when things in my life would start to get even worse I began to realize that what I was dealing with before wasn't all that bad.

I decided that even though I was still mad at God and didn't want to talk to Him that I would still do what He told me to do and go to the Christian bookstore to retrieve these items. Still, as I drove, I bitched about it and to Him the whole way there, "So that's how it's gonna be huh, You never help me when I'm in need, but You can manipulate my ass and play sick fuckin' mind games to get me to do Your work. Yes, I'm gonna do what You tell me to do and go to this stupid ass store; not because I give two shits about You, but because we both know that this is, an exchange for You to stop fuckin' with me!"

On the way there, I also complained about my car radio not working, and how I had to drive across town with no music. I shouted, "Wow, I get to spend the little bit of money I have for some stupid religious bullshit, but I can't even afford to get my fuckin' radio fixed or replaced. You're really on the ball today Oh Lord of the universe!" The people driving next to me were probably wondering who the guy next to them was that was yelling to himself. I shouted as I drove, "When this shit is over don't even fuckin' talk to me You fuckin' con artist, why do I always see more evidence of the devil in my life than You! The only time that I see evidence of You is when shit in my life is going bad."

Finally, I arrived at the Christian bookstore. I turned the car off and just looked at the building. I was so mad about being there and thought nobody better even try to give me any of that nice Christian bullshit because they could easily become a target for my attitude. I walked into the store and said to God, "Ok You phony God. What do You want me to buy today? Speak up bull-shitter." I walked around the store until I was shown what to grab. I mocked and put down the nice people I saw in there. When I would walk by someone, I would say under my breath, "You fuckin' idiot, wasting your money on this religious shit and all these lies." I was so full of anger that if I had touched one of the crucifixes in there, it probably would have burnt my skin. I said to God, "Ok let's hurry this up, what the fuck do You want me to buy?" God led me to pick up an N.I.V. Bible. When I took it up to the counter to pay for it, the cashier asked me if I wanted to have my name engraved on it. I said with a smart-ass attitude, "Wow you guys get the suckers coming and going don't you?" "No, it's free of charge and comes with the book," the cashier said with a smile on her face and not entertaining my negative emotional outburst. In retrospect, good for her. I heard God say, "Have Travis' name engraved on the Bible." "Fine, put the name Travis on there," I said. "It will take about ten minutes if you want to look around some more," she responded.

As I looked around the store some more, God began to show me other items to buy for Travis; a nice bookmark, some inspirational musical CD's, and to top it all off, a movie that I always enjoyed watching titled Jesus of Nazareth. Truth be told, I didn't know anything about Travis' religious or spiritual background or if he would even be receptive to the items I was buying for him. All I knew was that I was keeping my end of the deal with God, and if that meant He would stop making things hard on me then I would buy these items and give them to Travis, and he could burn them for all I cared.

I couldn't believe it; now I would be $60.00 in the hole. I couldn't afford these items at all, and I was pissed off about having to buy them. But if I didn't, God would allow the torment and negative things to continue to happen in my life. "You're a piece of shit," I said to God in disgust as I stood in the middle of this Christian bookstore. "At least with Satan, what you see is what you get. He doesn't have to play these sick manipulating mind games like Your ass does."

When my book was ready, I paid for all of the items and stormed out of the store. I opened the car door and just threw the bag on the passenger seat, not caring if I damaged the $60.00 worth of items I just purchased. I said, "There, I bought the stupid shit You wanted me to buy. Ya happy now Mr. Almighty great one? So now, what are You gonna do for me?" Instead of starting the car I just sat there in the driver's seat feeling angry about the money I had just spent. Then my anger began to turn to sadness. I was becoming emotional. The frustration was too much and was beginning to wear me down. I guess yelling at God didn't make me feel that much better. But I wasn't yelling at Him to make myself feel better, but because I was mad and felt forsaken. Then I quietly said, "I hate you."

After about ten minutes, I took the keys out of my pockets and put them in the ignition and when I started my car, something amazing happened - my radio came on. It was loud too! I couldn't believe it. After six months of silence, my radio was blaring loudly. Also, the song that was playing touched me directly to my heart, it was a song called "Seasons change" by the R&B pop group "Expose." God was letting me know through that title that what I was feeling and going through wasn't going to last and was just for a season and that seasons change. At that moment, I felt a little bit better on the inside. I didn't know what to think and still wasn't ready to forgive God or pretend that everything between us was cool just because He turned my radio on. Still, I drove home with a little bit of peace that somehow everything would be alright. I would get that confirmation when I walked into my apartment and saw the red light on my answering machine flashing. It was my supervisor; he said, "Anthony, we need you to come back to work. Can you fly out in two days?" Wow! My car radio came back on, and I was getting my job back all on the same day I chose to obey what God had told me to do. Imagine if I chose to continue to ignore Him?

Later that night while lying down, God spoke to me and He said "Do you not think that I know what you're going through in your life? If I can turn on your car stereo and give you your job back is there anything that I can't do for you if you're patient and wait for me?" I was humbled.

Travis was thankful for the items I purchased for him. Because of what I did, he went from being a man who had never stepped foot into a church in his life to becoming a loyal member of his church who never misses a service or meeting.

The reason people don't like or understand me is because I'm a real Godly person. I'm spiritually gifted and favored minded. I'm a unique individual, and my mentality and spirituality are on a higher level than most believers... Uh huh, I'm sure that's got to be the reason?

15

SOMETIMES ANGELS ARE JUST TESTING US

I have had so many situations where I've been tested by angels. These test usually come in the form of an angel/person needing help in some way. If there were other incidents and I'm sure there were, I just didn't realize it at the time.

Between the ages of eighteen to late twenties, I would continuously have experiences where someone in need approached me. They needed money; help lifting something heavy, directions, someone to talk to, or whatever the case would be. Sounds simple enough, right? But what made all of these experiences unique was all of the people in need usually had one thing in common, when they would approach me for any need of assistance, most of the time their physical appearances would fade in and out. Also, most of them would have the widest smiles on their faces, like they were happy just to be doing their spiritual jobs.

The first few times I witnessed this as an adult, I can't say that I was surprised or taken back by it. Like my mother, I was born with a natural instinct on spiritual matters. Also having grown up and experiencing other angel, spiritual and dark demonic entity's around my family and I, witnessing these types of occurrences wasn't strange or taboo to me as an adult. When angelic experiences would occur, I got so used to it that I would just roll my eyes and say, "Here we go again, what does this angel want now?" But I finally came to the conclusion that all of these experiences weren't just angels with nothing better to do, but that I was being tested. What other conclusions could I have come to? Would I help someone in need, or would I simply turn the other cheek?

In my early twenties, I was at work taking my half hour lunch break. I had a craving for a quarter pounder with cheese from the Mickey D's that was across the street. I had to hurry and be quick to make it back in time for work. I left work and ran all the way to the intersection. I witnessed a homeless man holding up a sign asking for money. Never on that side of town or at that intersection have I ever seen a homeless man begging for spare change, but today there he was. Then, the obvious happened. The closer I got to him the more his physical appearance would fade in and out. At that moment, I knew he wasn't an actual person but a spirit. Like I said, "Here we go again, what does this angel want now?" I stood next to him at the crosswalk, doing my best to ignore him and not get sucked into this trap or set up. I knew he didn't want money, and the spirit was there to test me.

He looked at me and smiled; I didn't smile back because I didn't want to be bothered, so I gave him a nod. I waited for the light to change and wanting to get away from this spirit as quickly as I could. That's when I heard God's voice, "Are you going to help this man or walk away from him?" By this point, the light had changed, but God's question kept me in my place. I responded to God and said, "We both know this man isn't real. I've been through this plenty of times before, so how can I be doing the right thing by helping this man if I already know he's a spirit?" God didn't respond, and that made the whole situation a little scary like He was upset at me for questioning Him. Hesitantly, I decided just to play along and give in to appease God. "I'm going to the McDonald's across the street, would you like me to bring you something back?" I asked the man. "A couple of burgers would be great," he responded. "No problem," I said. The light had changed again, and before I stepped off of the curb, I turned around and looked at the man, and said, "You're not going to be here when I get back are you?" He just smiled and shook his head no.

Sometimes when God is leading you to do something even if it doesn't make sense to you, such as buying hamburgers for a spirit, you just have to do it and trust that He's in control and has a meaning for everything. I learned a long time ago that there's power in obedience.

Of course, when I came back to the intersection, the homeless man/ spirit was nowhere to be found.

I always thought it was important to stop and smell the roses. I never thought to stop and thank God for creating them.

16

LITTLE OLD LADY AT THE LIBRARY

I was at the midtown library in the city of Anchorage. I had just finished using the computer and was making my way to the doors to leave the building. I decided to stop and get a Pepsi out of the soda machine. While I was standing near the machine and drinking my soda, I noticed a short old lady standing by the exit door. She was just staring through the glass motionless. I watched as people entered and exited the building without even acknowledging her and her not recognizing them. I just thought it was odd that such a fragile looking old lady was just standing there all by herself for no apparent reason.

I finished my soda, checked my voice messages, and made my way to the door. When I reached the door, the old lady turned and looked at me. She smiled at me and said, "Excuse me, it's very icy and slick outside, and I'm afraid I might fall. Will you please escort me to my car?" I thought it was odd, out of all of those people who walked by her she chose to say nothing, but to me, she asks this favor? Especially since I was looking like a thug that day. "Of course," I said, I smiled at her and gave her my arm.

While walking outside, I asked her where her car was. She pointed to an Olds Mobile that was across the parking lot in an area all by itself. That was fishy, because why would such an old fragile woman who has such a hard time walking on ice, park her car on the other side of a half empty parking lot when there are open handicapped spaces everywhere. I let the thought go and continued to walk her to her car.

When we reached her vehicle, I opened the door for her and helped her inside. She continuously thanked me. I closed her door, waved through the window and began to walk off. I got about twenty feet when I decided to turn around because I didn't hear her car start yet, to my surprise, the old lady and the car wasn't even there. At that moment, I knew it was just an angel testing me.

I guess sometimes it's easy to forget that just because we're under
man's law that God still has the final say and authority.

17

ANGELS IN THE COURTROOM

On a winter's afternoon, while driving, I was pulled over for running a red light by accident. Truth is, I don't ever remember running that red light at all, but the cop said I did. Then to make matters worse, I was driving without any insurance. The patrolling officer was friendly but still gave me two tickets and towed my vehicle. I was now due to appear in court.

At this point in my life, I had never been sent to court. I didn't know what the experience was like or how things worked. "Wouldn't it be great if this court was like the TV show 'Night Court' where everything was one big joke? The judge would be a funny guy, and the defendants would be hilarious characters," I thought to myself. When I arrived in the courtroom, it was the opposite of the humorous TV show. There were at least thirty or more defendants in the waiting area that were there for what seemed like the stupidest reasons. When they would go forward to be scolded by the judge, I couldn't help but think to myself, "Are you kiddin' me? This is what got you landed in court for?" It seemed like I was the only one there for a traffic offense. What I did didn't even seem half as bad as what these guys did. These defendants talked and joked amongst themselves as if they couldn't care less that they were in trouble or might have to pay a hefty fine or even get some jail time. If it were ten years earlier, I probably would have been laughing along with them. But at this particular age in my life and at that time, being in trouble with the law on any level was the last thing I wanted.

It seemed like it was taking forever for them to call my name. I was getting impatient and wanted to find out what my punishment was going to be. I was also amplifying my punishment in my head. Would I get a hefty fine I couldn't afford? Would I get some jail time? Or maybe long hours of community service? Sitting there doing nothing just gave my mind an excuse to wander.

I decided to do the only thing I could do to relieve my anxiety. I said a sincere prayer. Sitting in my seat, I lowered my head, and I said, "Father in heaven, I don't know what's going to happen here today, but You know I'm not a bad person, and I was on my way to work when I got pulled over on that morning. I've learned my lesson and feel that I shouldn't have to be punished too much by receiving jail time or paying a fine that I can't afford, and I don't have time to be picking up trash on the side of the highway. Please work it out for me, and also for these other defendants here as well, according to Your justice. I'll leave it in Your hands, amen." Even though my vehicle wasn't legit, God knew my heart was.

I opened my eyes. The courtroom seemed just a little brighter than before. The people around me were still whispering and talking; the judge continued to chastise the defendants, and the guards were stone-faced as if they were waiting for something dramatic to happen. That's when I saw a door in the front of the courtroom open up.

A man wearing a blue suit walked out of the room and walked towards the directions of the defendants sitting down. Out of all of us, he walked right up to me and said, "You… give me your paperwork." I handed him my tickets and paperwork. He looked at them for a moment, and said, "Don't worry about it. I'll take care of it, go home." Confused, I responded, "Go home?" He replied, "Yes, go home. You've nothing to worry about." With my paperwork in hand, he turned around and walked away. I couldn't help but to stop him and ask him, "Excuse me sir, but do I need some kind of paper or something saying that I was here, and I appeared in court?" I'll always remember what happened next. He stopped, turned around and looked at me with a smile; it was the big angelic smile that I had already become all too familiar. Calmly, he shook his head no and continued to walk away. At that moment, I knew to keep my mouth shut and do what I was told, "Go home!"

The problem with ignorant people is that they don't know that they're ignorant. But I'm learning.

18

MONEY FROM HEAVEN

I was working as a cook at a restaurant a while back when my supervisor told me I had a phone call. It was my mother. It was unusual for my mom to call me at work, so I was praying that it wasn't bad news and that everything was alright. Picking up the phone with my heart racing, I said, "Hey mom what's up?" She told me that she needed fifty dollars immediately to pay a bill. I told my mom that it was no problem, and I would get it to her A.S.A.P. After hanging up, I exhaled and was able to relax because it wasn't an emergency. But now I had another problem; I didn't have the fifty dollars at that time to give her.

The reason I didn't tell my mom that I didn't have the money was because when my mom says that she needs something, it's my job to tell her not to worry about it and figure out how to make it happen. That's what sons do. Still, I had to figure out how to get this money. I had just made payments on some of my loans and bills. And it would be a week and a half before I would see my next pay check. I hated having to borrow money from friends. So, how was I going to get the fifty dollars?

While I was thinking about ways to get the money, I started getting angry. At that time I was so sick and tired of always having to be a borrower instead of a lender. I hated that I could never catch up on bills. And when I started to get a little bit ahead, something would always come along to knock me backward. I thought working two jobs was the solution, but I was still behind on bills. Now, my mother needs fifty dollars, and I don't even have it to give to her. Some son I am who can't even give his mom money when she needs it.

Next, I did what I would usually do in these situations. I took my frustrations out on God. I asked him, "Why do I constantly bust my ass but I don't see any results or manifestations in my life? Things aren't getting better, and I don't see any doors opening or opportunity's happening for me. No matter how hard I work and sacrifice, my life never goes to another level. I'm working in this stupid kitchen, and now I can't even afford to help my mom when she needs me? Where's the love in that?" It had been a while since I spoke to God so passionately about my feelings but I have always been sensitive about my mother. That's why I lost my temper. I stopped my complaining and continued with my work.

A couple of hours had passed and I was still stewing in my own juices. Then, something out of the ordinary happened. One of the servers came into the kitchen and approached me. This particular server never spoke to me before except an acknowledgment in passing. At that time I didn't even know her name. I called her tattoo because her body was covered in tattoos that she hid by wearing long sleeve shirts and turtle necks. She held her hand out to me and gave me forty-five dollars. I was shocked and asked, "What's this for?" She said, "We have a lot of church idiots eating here tonight. There must be some religious convention in town or something. Anyway, one of the ladies asked me who the cook was that made her steak. I had forgotten your name, but she told me to give this money to you." I replied, "She gave you forty-five dollars to give to me?" She said, "Yea, that's more than her meal cost (laughing) church folks are all strange to me that's why I don't go." It wasn't enough to just take the money; this lady really helped me out at a time when I desperately needed it. I asked Tattoo to point the lady out to me so I could thank her personally.

We walked to the dining area, but the lady wasn't sitting at the table. I asked Tattoo to look in the bathroom, but she wasn't in there either. Tattoo asked the people sitting at the twenty-seven seat table what happened to the lady who was sitting in that particular chair. One of the men responded that the only person who was sitting in that seat was his brother. She then asked where the lady was who was just sitting at the table that gave her money to give to the cook who had made her steak. None of the women at the table took accountability for the large tip and Tattoo didn't recognize any of the ladies as the one who gave her the money. I could see that Tattoo was getting a little annoyed and felt a little ridiculed, but since she was one of the servers at the table, she did her best to keep a professional demeanor. I realized that it could have been an angel that God had planted there to help me, but Tattoo wouldn't understand that. I pulled her to the side and said, "Don't worry about it, no big deal." I could see that she felt a little embarrassed. She said, "I don't know where she is, but she was here at this table in this seat. Maybe she left?"

Of course, I knew where the money really came from. I thanked Tattoo and walked back into the kitchen, got on one knee and thanked God for the money. Even though I was bitching and complaining before, instead of turning His back on me, He helped me. After work when I walked out to my car, next to the driver's door was a puddle of water. Floating on top of the water face down was a five dollar bill. I had received the fifty dollars in full. "Thank you, Father in heaven."

A person's negative attitude toward us doesn't make them our enemy. But how we choose to think and respond toward that person can make us our own enemy.

19

THE BULLY

My eighth-grade year 1987/88, I attended Central junior high school in Anchorage, Alaska. The school student majority was mostly made up of minority students who were military brats. I came to school in the middle of the year and quickly learned that the students there were more concerned with the latest fashion, footwear, hairstyles, latest music and dances. Sure most junior high and high schools were like this, but this particular school was out of control with its fads. Still, I was cocky, arrogant, good looking and had more knowledge than the students and teachers that attended and worked there. I also had all of the answers and the meaning of life figured out. Yes, I was one of those teenagers.

I fit right in and had no problem with the girls. Every day I would open my locker to find love letters that were slipped into it by girls telling me how fine and hot I was and hoping I would choose them to be my girlfriend. I enjoyed the attention I was getting and envied by most of the other guys at the school. I had girls so much on my mind to the point to where I neglected my school work and studies. I spent more time in the bathroom mirror than I did in class. Even though I was the gift sent from heaven for most of these girls at this school, for another girl named Rita, I was her nightmare from hell.

Rita was a dark skinned sista who I shared a social studies class with. She was a nice, sweet Christian girl. She never swore or said anything bad about anybody. She always had a smile on her face, and our social studies teacher just adored her. She got good grades, had a good attendance record and was a model student. For me, she was just ripe enough as a target for a good clown session. While in class I never missed an opportunity to call her a name, make fun of something she was wearing, mock her conversations she would have with the other girls in the class, or try to point out something about her I didn't like to get the whole class to laugh at her. For Rita, sharing a class with me was horrible. These verbal attacks against her went on daily and for the remainder of the school year and she deserved none of it. Rita had never offended me in any way or had never done anything bad to me, so why did I make her my target for teasing? I had never treated another student or classmate the way I treated her. One day our teacher even pulled me out of class and into the hall and asked me what my problem was with Rita. She also threatened to have me suspended if I didn't stop teasing her. Still, I continued doing it, just behind her back. If I had to guess why I put out this negative behavior towards Rita, it would be because subconsciously I was lashing out about how unhappy I was at home and I made her my target to unleash my frustrations on. At that time, my house wasn't a very happy or stable home. There was no structure, head of the house, discipline, and in some cases food. My Brother Mark and I were full-time thieves who stole cars, robbed houses and even the neighborhood church for food and money. I won't go into detail about it, but I will say that I made it a point to stay the night at my friend's houses whenever I could so that I could have a hot meal. Deep down I was an unhappy teenager.

What's even worse is at the time I didn't even know the degree of how I was making Rita feel with my behavior. I thought I was just being me, a stupid pretty boy teenager who was trying to be funny all the time to get attention. In the end, all I did was make her eighth-grade year a horrible experience for her, to the point where almost daily she would go home crying to her mother about the way I was treating her. Her mother would say to her, "Maybe that boy just has a crush on you, and that's why he picks on you." She dreaded coming to class with me because instead of focusing on her school work she was consumed with what I was going to say to her next. I always delivered. After the school year had ended, she went on to high school, and it would be years before I would ever see her again.

In my early twenties, I started a rap group called "Dirty Livin." I was working hard to make sure my group was a success by booking shows and airing TV/radio commercials to advertise our latest tape. At this point in my life making it big in the business was the only thing that consumed my mind. One afternoon I went to one of the local Kinko's to get some flyers made for one of our upcoming shows. I approached a woman sitting at a desk to ask her for some information. When I saw who it was, I was a little surprised and taken back, it was Rita. "Wow," I thought, "I haven't seen her since I was fourteen." She looked lovely, confident and kept a professional demeanor. I wondered if she even remembered who I was. Do you ever forget the person who teased you in school? I think not. I asked her for her assistance, and she guided me on what I was to do to get my flyers designed. I believed she remembered me, but she didn't let on or show any body language that said otherwise. She just assisted me, and I went on about my business.

As the weeks went by I couldn't get the run in I had with Rita out of my head. I thought about how pretty she looked, so grown up and without really knowing her I could tell that she was still the great person she was in junior high, always ready to be there and help someone. I wondered how she was doing and what her life was like at that time. Was she married? Did she have a family? What hobbies did she have? Even at night, I found myself consumed with thinking about her since our brief meeting at her job. After awhile, I began to question myself, "Why am I thinking about Rita all the time? Why can't I get this woman out of my head? Am I becoming attracted to her because she's so pretty now, and I'm just caught up in the idea of her because I haven't seen her in a long time? Am I trying to convince myself that running into her was meant to be or is God trying to tell me something?" Thoughts raced back and forth in my mind about why I was overwhelmed with thoughts of Rita. I would get my answer. I didn't know it at the time, but God was showing me why I was constantly thinking about Rita, it was guilt! Guilt for the way I treated that poor girl in junior high school, and He also showed me that nothing was going to put out that fire except a sincere apology for my behavior towards her.

Of course, I knew that God was right, and it was the right thing for me to do, but still I didn't have the guts to face Rita to apologize. When you know that you've wronged somebody and they probably have a bad taste in their mouth about you, it's not always easy to try to get them to see you in another light. I felt like even if I did apologize to her, she probably doesn't want to hear it and would just hear me out to be polite.

I put it off for a while and tried to make up excuses to myself for not apologizing such as, "Oh, that was a long time ago I'm sure she's over it by now" or "she probably doesn't even remember me." A couple of months had gone by and the more I put it off, the stronger the Holy Spirit convicted me to the point to where I finally had to give in, man up, and take my sorry ass back to her job and apologize to this wonderful Christian woman for my behavior in the past.

The big day came. I finally arrived at her job; I was ready to apologize and even face rejection from her. I approached the counter; nervously I asked if Rita was working that day, the man behind the counter said, "Rita no longer works here." At that moment, all of the energy left my body as I stood in a slumping position. Never have I felt so relieved and disappointed at the same time. I felt like I had gotten away with it because I didn't have to go through with it, but at the same time, I felt like I had lost because I didn't get to go through with it. I decided that if I ran into her on the street or at the grocery store, I would apologize to her, but other than that I was going to put this behind me and move on.

As the years went by and I was in my mid-thirties, I would find myself thinking about Rita and wondering how she was doing every so often. My guilt for her was still apparent and deep down I still wanted the chance to apologize to her. I would even say a prayer for her from time to time. In these prayers I would say to God, "Please Father in heaven, please watch over Rita and please create an opportunity for me to apologize to her, You give the word, and it will be done. Amen." I still felt guilty about the way I treated her in the past and missing my chance to apologize to her weighed heavy on my heart. "If I could just apologize to her, I could close that chapter in my life," I felt, but I didn't even know how it would happen or under what circumstances. I doubt she even still lives in Alaska because the majority of my class has already moved out of the state.

One afternoon I found myself being curious about this new website that everyone was talking about called Face book. I decided to jump on the bandwagon and create an account on the site, only because I was told that it was a good way to advertise and update people about projects that involved me. I never had any real plans on using it as a means to catch up with old friends, but that's what it turned out to be anyway. After I had set up my account, I decided that I was tired and would add my pictures the next day. I plopped on the couch to watch some TV. While watching a movie on the Spike channel, there was a woman in the movie who looked just like Rita to me. So much so that after awhile of watching this woman on the screen I became overwhelmed with the guilt of past thoughts of my behavior towards her. I thought to myself, "How could I have treated her so poorly?" After about fifteen minutes of feeling like crap, I felt convicted to pray for her, so I got on my knees and began to pray to God harder about this Rita situation than I ever had before. I begged God for the chance to apologize to her very soon because I needed to do this for me. I poured my heart and soul into that prayer because again I really needed to close that chapter amongst other chapters once and for all in my life. That's when it hit me like a ton of bricks. Instantly, God had shown me something, an impression; God had opened my heart to what my real problem was and why He hadn't opened another door for me to apologize to Rita. I didn't realize this before, but God had revealed to me that I only wanted to apologize to Rita to relieve my guilt, not once did I ever considered how I truly made her feel or what I really put her through. I was only concerned with making myself feel better about the situation; that's why God hadn't given me another chance to tell her I'm sorry. I needed to apologize to her because she was a good person who didn't deserve any of my verbal abuse and all the hell I put her through. He told me not to worry about how I feel or about my guilt and redemption.

I was thankful that God had shown that to me, but now that I know this about myself, what am I supposed to do with this new information? After all, I can't fix what I can't catch. That night as I began to drift off to sleep I mustered up enough energy to ask God for another chance to apologize to Rita, and, "This time, I won't blow it, I promise."

The next day after running errands I decided to sit at the computer and add some pictures to my Face book account. I logged on, and when my home page came up, I was floored by what I saw next. It was a picture of Rita. Next to her picture it said, "Someone you may know." I couldn't believe it, God had heard my prayer and had answered it fast. He knew that once I understood where I had error, He could move forward in helping me do what I needed to do and not a moment too soon. Once again God had given me a chance to apologize to Rita.

I waited for a couple of days before actually writing her a letter. I thought about what I would say. I wanted to make sure that I didn't forget anything, but when I sat down and wrote the letter of apology and asking her for her forgiveness, I realized that the hardest part wasn't writing the letter, but when I was done, the hardest part for me was pushing the send button. I wondered, "Does Rita even want to hear from me and will she accept my apology after twenty years?" I had to remind myself that this wasn't about me or my feelings, but it's about doing the right thing towards Rita. I pushed the send button.

As the next few days went by, I remember being scared to check my email because she just might write me back with an ugly letter or she might not write me back at all. Either way, I was nervous. Then finally, I got a response from Rita. I was scared to open the message. I stared at the computer screen for what felt like an eternity. But I knew whether she accepted my apology or not I did the right thing. I apologized to her. Finally, I opened the message. I began to smile as I read it. Not only did she accept my apology and was thankful for it, but it turned out that she was the same sweet, awesome, caring, giving, loving, Christian (and now a mother of two) woman that she had always been. Amen!

We exchanged phone numbers, and I can still remember being nervous to call her. But when I did call, it was great. We were like teenagers all over again. We talked and laughed about old school days and people we remembered, and we became good friends. She even helped me emotionally, been there for me through some tough times and had even given me spiritual encouragement on more than one occasion when I really needed it. Never in my entire life have I ever seen so much devotion to God from an individual. She is madly in love with the Lord. Life is funny and sometimes the Lord has a way of working things out that we don't always see. I would have never thought that the girl who I once teased in junior high school, as adults, would be uplifting me and given me encouragement, and I would be someone she would be happy to call her friend. I am blessed to have her in my life and can call her my friend.

Thank you Rita.

Thank you Father in heaven.

We can never be smart, intelligent, brilliant or a genius.
But we can be ignorant on a higher level.

20

GOD ALREADY KNOWS ALL OF THE ANSWERS. ALL YOU HAVE TO DO IS ASK HIM

I decided I wanted to make a little more money by becoming a truck driver and also to add to my work resume. I couldn't afford to pay for the trucking class I wanted to attend, so I decided to try to get a grant to pay for the class, and that meant attending the classes and courses of a particular agency to receive this money. I attended their class for two weeks, listened to their lectures, and the teachers and counselors talked to the students like they were stupid adults who were beneath them. The procedure was annoying and a little brutal. Still, they had the money I needed to go to another level and if I had to put up with a little rudeness and bad attitudes to get to where I was trying to go then so be it.

It was the last day of class, and I got through the course without having to lose my cool or go off on anybody. Of course, I'm talking about the arrogant staff members. I still didn't know if I was even going to be able to receive any money at all from these people because they wouldn't tell us that far an advance until the classes were finished. There were only three hours left of the last day. I was feeling pretty good knowing that even if I didn't receive any money from them, I would at least be done with having to come back to this place. Then, the teacher walked in and dropped another bomb on us. He said he was giving us a math test, and if we failed the test, we failed the entire course and would have to come back in four months to take it all over again. The whole class was stunned. I was so pissed off and couldn't believe that they would wait until the last day to drop this make it or break it math test on us without even telling us about it from the beginning. It left a bad taste in everybody's mouth.

I have never had school smarts. Math and I were the worst of enemies. I can honestly say that at this very moment if you were to put a two digit division problem in front of me I would struggle with it and would still probably get it wrong. However, I had no real choice other than taking the test. While passing out the tests the teacher told us, the test was trigonometry and algebra problems. Also, the class that took the test before us had almost forty students in it and only three students passed the test. He seemed exceedingly happy about it as if he were some kind of puppet master who took pride in demeaning and looking down on his students instead of trying to help them.

I just sunk into my chair. I was filled with anger and depression at the same time. I began breathing heavy through my nose and closed my fist and softly pounded it on my desk twice. I spoke to God and decided to take my frustrations out on Him. I said, "God, why did You bring me this far in this class so that I could fail in the end. You know I don't know anything about math, and I'm dyslexic. I thought You were helping me. In the previous class only three out of forty people passed, how do You think I'm supposed to pass this test?" I stopped talking to God and just stared at the multiple choice thirty question test that might as well been written in a foreign language. Then, God spoke to me; His voice was loud and clear when He said, "Do you just want to sit there and be mad at Me, or do you want to ask Me for My help?" I clearly understood what He was saying. I also felt that even though I couldn't see how I could pass this test even with His help, that this was God's way of wanting to show off and show His love for me. Sarcastically, with a little bit of an attitude, I said to Him, "Ok God, I don't know what I'm doing, and I don't know the answers to any of these math problems. Will You please guide my hand and fill in the correct answers for me. I really need to pass this test and get this money so I can attend truck driving school. Please help me." I took a deep breath and stared at the page. I couldn't make heads or tails of what I was looking at so I cleared my mind and imagined that Jesus was in the room standing next to me. I repeated myself to God and said, "Please Father, guide my hand and fill in the correct answers for me." Without even knowing what the questions were I began to fill in the circles. Some answers were A, some,

B, C, and D. I just imagined in my head that God put His hand over my hand and was controlling and guiding it. I gave my math problems to Him. When the time had run out, I came back to my reality and began worrying again. Thinking I had failed miserably, I turned in my complete but insincere test. We were instructed to sit in the waiting area until they called our name for the results. Knowing I didn't even read the questions and just filled in the answers I was already preparing myself for the worst. "I guess I'll be coming back to this stupid school in four months to do this all over again, damn I'm depressed."

After an hour of waiting, the man finally called my name to come up for my test results. He just looked at me and said, "You'll need to come back here next Monday to speak to your case worker." "I don't get it, what does that mean?" I asked. "Well, she's going to start the process of getting your money for your schooling," he responded. Confused I said, "I don't get it, are you saying I passed the math test?" "Yea, you only got three wrong," he responded. I said out loud, "Three wrong?" I was dumbfounded. Out of thirty questions of trigonometry and algebra problems that I didn't even read the questions to and wouldn't even know what I was reading if I did, I only got three answers wrong. All because I relaxed my mind and asked God to guide my hand and to fill in the correct answers for me. He came through.

I was so happy about passing my test that I was showing everybody as I was walking towards the front door. At that moment, I saw a woman, a sista, from my class sitting at a table waiting for her test results and looking a little down. I asked her what was wrong, and she said that she knew that she had failed the test because it was too hard and she had never done math like that before. She said that she needed the grant money so she could get into school. She had two kids, wanted to start a new life and to take care of her children. I felt for her and her sadness. I told her I would sit with her until they called her for her test results.

For the next hour, the sad woman and I talked and shared things about ourselves and our pasts. I even managed to make her smile a little bit and keep her mind off of the test results. Then I heard God's voice speak to me again. He asked me, "Why are you just talking to her when you should be praying for her?" I understood, and began to pray for her "Father, please help this woman, You know what her needs are and that she's just trying to make a better life for herself and her kids. Please, please, please help her and let her pass her test so she can go to the next level of the program. She really needs You right now." I sincerely prayed that prayer at least five times in between our conversations. Finally, she was called up to the window. She gave me a scared look, got up and held her head low as she walked to the counter. With every step she took, I prayed even harder. I watched her speaking to the man as she stood at the window. Then, her face lit up. She screamed and covered her mouth at the same time. She turned around and gave me the nod of approval. She passed! She had no clue as to how she passed that math test, but I knew. Sometimes you have to ask the One who knows all of the answers. "Thank You, Father in heaven for helping that woman and myself. That was all You."

There are two types of people in the world, God's children and God's children.

21

THE WOMAN ON
THE SIDEWALK

Ever since I was a little boy, I've always been a big Kiss fan. Growing up in the late 70's and early 80's my whole world revolved around Kiss. I bought all their records and magazines that featured the band. My room was plastered with Kiss posters. There was something about the makeup, outrageous outfits and the live show that was like a rock and roll circus that really captured my imagination. Today you have movies, TV shows, and wrestlers who wear makeup or have a crazy look about them but back when I was growing up these real-life characters rarely existed, except for Kiss. In my young eyes, they weren't just a rock band, they were real life superheroes.

In 2012, I found out that Kiss would be playing at the Mandalay Bay in Las Vegas. Currently living in Las Vegas, I was looking forward to going to this concert to see my childhood heroes once again on stage, and this would be my fourth Kiss concert. Sure they don't move as fast as they used to and sometimes the wigs look a little funny. They'll sometimes forget the lyrics to their own songs, but for men in their mid sixties, they still put on an amazingly energetic live concert experience.

At this time I had never been to the Mandalay Bay and was miss informed when I was told that it seats up to thirty thousand people. Having heard that, I figured I had more than enough time to buy my ticket for the show, so I put the subject aside until it was closer to the day of the show.

By the time August had rolled around there had been enough hype and talk about the concert to where I decided I shouldn't put it off anymore and purchase my ticket to secure a seat. When I arrived at the Mandalay

Bay box office, I got some horrific news. The Kiss concert was sold out! Instantly I had a lump in my throat, and it sank to my stomach. The clerk informed me that the arena didn't seat thirty thousand but only twelve thousand people for sporting events. For concerts, it only held nine thousand. After kicking myself in the ass over the next few days for missing an easy opportunity, I came to the conclusion that my only options were to buy a ticket off Craigslist or try to buy one from a scalper on the day of the show.

Trying to buy a ticket online didn't work, and most of the seller's asking prices were through the roof. Some sellers never even called me back even when I told them that I would meet them at a certain time and location to buy a ticket. I suppose they found other buyers who would meet their asking price. I gave up on the online sellers and realized that I would have to place all of my hopes on a ticket scalper hours before show time.

The morning of the concert I woke up alert, focused and ready. My only function that day was to buy my Kiss ticket and nothing else. Like the Terminator, I was programmed to my objective and nothing was going to sway me otherwise, so I thought.

Hours before the show, I was showered, dressed and ready for battle. I grabbed the items that I was taken with me and walked out the door. I decided to walk the half hour distance to the show to avoid traffic and to have to find a place to park. I made it about a block when I heard God speak to me, "Go back home!" I thought, "Why is God telling me to go back home?" I ignored the order and because I was in such a hurry, I decided to chalk it up to my imagination. I put my mind back to focus mode and walked two more blocks when I would hear God's voice again, "Go back home!" This time, it was more demanding. I wondered, "Why is God telling me to go back home? What was the big emergency? Did I leave the stove on? Did I forget something?" It really annoyed me, but I decided just to listen and go back home. I was cussing with every footstep. This was interrupting my plan to get a Kiss ticket, and I was losing time.

I made it back to my apartment and looked around to make sure that everything was in place, and the stove was off. I doubled checked to make sure that I had all of the items I needed including my driver's license in case the Mandalay Bay wanted I.D. I wondered, "What the hell?" I asked, "God why did You send me back here?" I assumed I was just trippin' because of my nerves about having to still get a concert ticket for the show. Feeling like I had wasted my time coming back home and that God really wasn't speaking to me, I headed for the door. Before I could grab the handle, I looked to my left and saw a small booklet on the chair. It was a pocket size Christian book on the healing powers of God and scripture. Sometimes I would mail order CD sermons of certain preachers, and I would get small gifts from these churches like a small book or a free bookmark. The truth is, I don't even remember putting it on the chair, but there it was. I didn't know why, but I just stared at the book on the chair, and that's when I knew that this small book was the reason why I was sent back home. What purpose it was going to serve I didn't know or try to figure it out. I had a Kiss concert to get to, and I had to get back in focus. I put the small book in my pocket. I quickly ran out the door and walked even faster to make up for lost time. Whatever it takes, I wasn't missing this concert. You would think at this age I would have outgrown Kiss or even be able to put this whole Kiss fan thing in perspective. But even as an adult there has always been something about Kiss that always brings out the late 70's fan in me.

Walking through the Las Vegas streets, I was surrounded by fanatics also on the way to the show, wearing Kiss makeup and costumes from different eras. A couple who had just gotten married wearing Kiss makeup was throwing cigars out of the sunroof of their limo. Other fans were standing on the street corners with their guitars playing Kiss songs to get the already excited fans blood rushing even more. As for me, I was totally jealous of every one of these nut-jobs, because I knew as weird and as fanatical as they were, they had Kiss tickets in their pockets and I didn't.

I was only a block away from the Mandalay Bay, and my heart was racing even more. I began hunting for scalpers in the area or anybody holding a sign that said, "Kiss tickets for sell." Walking down the sidewalk, I noticed I was approaching a hippy looking woman sitting cross-legged on the ground. She didn't exactly look homeless but at the same time, she looked like she was struggling in life with her unkempt clothing and hair. When I walked past her, she looked at me with a "no matter what happens in life everything is going to be ok" smile. Then, she spoke to me and said, "How are you sir?" It was weird. With that simple question, she sounded sincere, not at all did it sound like a mere attempt for small talk nor that she wanted anything from me. This stranger with this great smile honestly wanted to know how I was doing. The problem was I had a mission to buy a Kiss ticket and wasn't interested in feeble small talk. Without missing a step, I arrogantly responded, "Great," and kept walking past her.

I was approaching a crosswalk at a busy intersection when I spotted a man across the street holding a sign that said, "Kiss tickets for sell." At this point, I didn't care what his asking price was; I just had to have a ticket. I kept my eye on him to make sure he didn't walk away, and no one else got to him before I did. Finally, the walk signal came on, still keeping my eye on him, something weird happened, I couldn't walk. I mean my body actually couldn't go forward. My feet felt like I was wearing thousand pounds boots made out of cement, they wouldn't move. I started to feel nauseous and the more I struggled to go forward the more ill I felt, and the more heavier my body became and my feet stayed planted to the ground. Then, I heard God say to me, "Go back and speak to that woman!" In my unauthorized submissive state, I tried to argue with God that I couldn't, and I had to get to the man across the street with the Kiss tickets for sell. God didn't respond to my reasoning. I also saw that this was a battle that He was going to win. Still, I gave it one last effort and tried to go forward; again my body wouldn't move. I decided to give up and realized what I had to do. Listen to God and go back and talk to that woman. Not only that, but the faster I go back and speak to the woman the faster I can get back to my business.

Frustrated, I walked back to the strange woman who was sitting on the ground still smiling and spoke to her, "Hey, I'm sorry if I was rude when I walked past you. I was just in a hurry and wasn't really thinking. But again, I'm sorry if I came off as an ass." At first, she just looked at me and smiled; her demeanor said, "Whether you talk to me or not, we're still friends and children of God." Never have I felt so humbled and ashamed at the same time by just some woman looking at me but there I was. "Don't even worry about it," she said, "I can see you're in a hurry." I really didn't know what to say to her or why God sent me back to her. Was it because I was rude and needed to apologize to her? Well, I already did that, but was that it? I said the only thing I could think of "So, are you ok." What she said next blew me away, "Yea, I'm ok because I believe I'm ok. I have a life threatening illness in my body, but I'm not worried because every day I ask God for healing. I know He hears me. I've never been to church or even read the Bible, but I know who God is, and He knows me. I know in my heart God loves me." With those few words she spoke I was so impressed with her faith. I know plenty of people who do go to church and regularly read their Bibles who didn't have half of this woman's faith, and that includes me. She had a life-threatening illness, and she's still standing her ground and believing in God with a big smile on her face. Selfishly, my biggest concern at that moment was buying a concert ticket? Boy, I felt two feet tall. It was at that moment that I realized why God had sent me back home to pick up that small book on the healing powers of Him and scripture; He wanted me to give it to her. In my mind, I said, "I know, Father, I know." I told her I had something for her and pulled out the small book. When she saw that it was a book on healing her eyes began to tear, she said to me, "See, God sends me signs like this all the time, I told you God knows me, I know He loves me."

After talking to her, I was no longer in a hurry. I slowly walked away and thought about the faith I had just witnessed. I got my concert ticket and that night, even though I was staring at my childhood heroes on stage, I couldn't stop thinking about the woman on the sidewalk and her faith.

22

JUST CALL ON HIS NAME

It was a cold, snowy day in Anchorage, Alaska. I was driving my car in a blizzard, and the streets were covered in a glaze of ice. I was driving faster than I probably should have on the ice but I was running late for work and was trying to make up some time by going over the speed limit.

My right turn was coming up. I lightly tapped my breaks to slow down, and before I knew it, I had lost control of my car and began sliding.

Another vehicle had pulled up to the stop sign where I was turning right, and I was sliding fast directly towards it. I was bug-eyed and frozen. The driver in front of me and I were locked in eye-to-eye contact; I could see he too was bug-eyed, and neither of us had time to react.

I didn't plan on saying it and God and Jesus was the last thing on my mind. But without even thinking about it I yelled out the name, "Jesus!"

At that very moment, I felt my car being lifted up off the ground, turned and positioned into the turning lane I was trying to enter. The other driver and I never even touched each other.

Just like that I called on the name "Jesus" and was saved from a collision. I had no time to say a prayer or even think. All I could do was call on His name; that's it, and the power of just calling on His name saved me.

I don't know who the other driver was, but I'm sure even to this day he is still dumbfounded by the fact that a car that was barreling down on him was mysteriously lifted up off the ground and moved out of his way.

THANK YOU

I want to thank you for taking the time to purchase this book and reading it. I'm grateful and happy to be able to share my experiences with you. These experiences have been over a lifetime, but sometimes they seem like yesterday.

I wanted to let you know that He is always working in your life. You don't realize it, but He sends thousands of angels daily to protect you, guide you, and to watch over you so that you can fulfill the purpose He has for you. He is interested in having a close personal relationship with you. He just doesn't want to be your God: He wants to be your Father as well.

He is not hiding anything from you, including Himself. More than anything, your Father in heaven wants to reveal Himself to you today. He wants to hold you and to love you. He wants to take away your fears, doubts, and uncertainty. He wants to bring your mind and heart into His peace. Let Him.

He doesn't care what you've done or what sins you've committed. He doesn't care how broken you are or how other people see you. He wants you to come to Him whether you're mentally, emotionally unbalanced, dirty, abused or tired. He wants you to come to Him as you are. You're not waiting on Him - He's waiting on you.

Printed in the United States
By Bookmasters